Flyover State

Hoosier stories from the heartland

Nick O'Neill

ISBN: 978-0-578-33593-3

Table of Contents

Acknowledgements

A very wise woman once told me, "If people don't like what you have written, maybe they should've behaved differently." This has proven to be the very best advice anyone has ever given me about writing; just write. Stop worrying about what people will think. Just open yourself up and bleed onto the page. Obviously, some details have been smudged, altered, or even downright removed to save the fragile egos of very fallible, mortal souls – but this is art, not fact. This is… a dance, not a march. This is a big-mouthed, malcontent button pusher regurgitating a few little nuggets of Midwestern American "wisdom" through a very distorted and admittedly hazy looking glass into the past and present conditions that define just one life in an ocean of billions of others. So… I wrote them down. Take them as you will.

My goal for this collection was to make people think, take a mental deep breath, or at the very least – just smile. If this has been your experience along the journey, then it is also thanks to the motley crew below that anything was ever accomplished towards this endeavor.

First and foremost, this book is dedicated to Paula - a much beloved public high school English teacher who has taught me everything worth knowing about legacy. Your light will shine in the minds and hearts of the thousands of souls you have guided through your decades of public service long after you've left us all here to contemplate those lessons without you. You are the living personification of true instruction, guidance, and encouragement. If my treasure in life is my trove of friends, then you are by far the crown jewel of the collection. The world is a better place because you are in it. Thank you.

Second, to another public-school English teacher and angel named Sarah, this book is also dedicated to you. I remember missing my chance to study under you and lamenting my misfortune at the beginning of my high school experience, only to land in your American Literature class a mere two years later. You introduced us to the writings of Henry David Thoreau, Ralph Waldo Emerson, Arthur Miller, Eugene O'Neill… and countless others who opened my eyes to the experience of the human condition through an American perspective, free of politics and pressure and the modern interpretation of such a controversial label. Oh, how I miss those classes! Our freedom to share quotes of personal import on the classroom whiteboard, free of scorn and ridicule and punitive strike. Our freedom to dislike, challenge, debate, and then absorb true knowledge is as priceless today as it was those many years ago. Your life today continues to bless so many of us in so many ways with your nature photography, your poetic words, and your smile. The world is a better place because you are in it. Thank you.

To Amie: I am unlikely to find another friend in my life who has challenged and/or aided me as you have for many years. This book would quite literally have been impossible without your efforts. The world is a better place because you are in it. Thank you.

Finally, I would like to thank my family and friends for their patience, their love, and oddly enough for their all-too-relatable talent for miscalculation, mistakes, and existential fragility. I have only begun to download my lifetime of madness onto the page, and none of it would be possible to reproduce if I were surrounded by boring, hollow souls. I gave up on the illusion of perfection long ago, but the only world to be in is one I have to share with you. The world is the only place to be because you are in it. Thank you.

Foreword

Wordsmithing is a lonely pursuit.

When I was in grade school and then in college, I found it impossible to study or complete homework with any sonic or visual distractions within any minor proximity of my sphere of existence. The maelstrom that is the inner sanctum of my brainbucket is chaos unhinged, and I have often compared my thought process to plucking random debris from the unrelenting, tornadic malaise that is my inner monologue/cognitive immolation.

This perturbed condition is rarely aided by technology, other humans, animals, or anything but the random chance of quiet moments for reflection; organizing my teetering moments of clarity onto the page and praying at least some of what I write makes any sense to anyone whatsoever. These moments are fleeting. Priceless and rare. And require at least twice the effort to edit and organize than they ever do to initially produce

The illustrations you see in this book are a literal representation of my mental maddening condition – every one of them was born of moments where I was supposed to be doing something else. College lectures. Waiting on hold with customer service/technical support. Meetings. Sermons. Appointments. They are the product of a wiggling hand, a distraction-tempted mind, and a teeth-gnashing resistance to lost time's stolen potential. The editing process to transform them from lined pages into digital flair was also a battle royale, but I felt them important enough to share. The glyphs feel good to release.

For the record - I do not recommend a subscription to this random mental method, if at all possible. It rips time away as a ravenous Tyrannosaur rending flesh from a Stegosaur thigh bone. It steals moments and magic and meaning from so many otherwise worthwhile pursuits.

But every once in a while, the storm clouds part. The wind picks up, and there is music to be found in the madness.

This collection is a celebration of those notes that span decades of a life otherwise well-wasted in a part of the country that is better known as the butt of any given hayseed joke than for its humanity. These are stories from the heartland told by a true Hoosier.

Part One: Observing

I've heard it said that artists and writers have the gift of seeing the world, debatably life itself, through a unique set of lenses. Rose-colored glasses, blinders, fogged binoculars… whatever the alteration, I would tend to agree. We sometimes have trouble blending in, fitting in, disappearing into the teeming masses while quietly, defiantly living our lives by anyone else's code but our own. But I humbly admit that most of what I see and hear is probably as far from the entire truth as any single soul could ever witness.

This isn't always by choice; often the perspective has to be unique because the circumstances themselves are unique. Other times all it takes is a bit of imagination… and madness… to make the "all day, every day" something even slightly extraordinary.

The first section of this book is a collection created in that very spirit.

Looking at nature.

Looking at ourselves.

Looking.

FLIGHT OF THE CHICKIE-BOCK-BOCKS

Being a professional I.T. nerd has its advantages. Never at a want for company, the slightest suggestion of a source for our often-quiet nature arouses those with computer or technological device challenges to rush towards us like religious fanatics at a Charlton Heston fandom convention (see: Cecil B DeMille's Ten Commandments — Blu-Ray Disc #2). We enshroud ourselves in mystery for good reason — just as mechanics, doctors, dentists, lawyers, mutants, superheroes, wizards, and other unfortunate populace-serving souls who are similarly bum rushed when their true identities are revealed. Giving out free advice or service can lead one to social and societal burnout faster than, well, fried chicken gets served in Kentucky.

Since I was a boy, I have loved fried chicken. "Drumsticks" may mean something different to those of you with band and percussion backgrounds, but for me? Even now my mouth is watering remembering the glory that was a lifetime of relishing my mother's fried-chicken-and-mashed-potatoes-with-gravy dinners that made me the man-and-a-half I am today. Cholesterol? Don't care. Fat? Don't care. Sodium? Don't care. One bite and it was the rebirth of my soul into the realm of exquisite oral nirvana. Heavenly juicy deliciousness, hallowed be thy plate.

In adulthood, I admit that chicken tends to be a staple that never ceases to entice me. Chicken sammiches, nuggies, roasted and broasted, broiled and rotisserie'd, giblets and gizzards and livers and thighs, spicy or juicy or noodle-ized, it is hard for me to turn down the bird. In fact, it's hard for me to turn down multiple servings of these meatlings in any sitting.

However, I am now confronted with a different perspective on these creatures:

The chorale in question was not unfamiliar to me. In fact, I've noticed them every trip I make outdoors for weeks now. I regarded them as the source for fresh eggs for my family relations, but little more. I thought they were content to live out their lives in their coop, until such matters of age and proper hunger would dictate a proper end to such a noble charge: nourish my family with their eggs and maybe one day eventually their very bodies. I did not ask my relation if they had names, if they had personalities, or even how many or how old they were. I relegated them to the boutique, trendy, first-world middle class curiosity that is saving a couple of bucks at the grocery store and inheriting a coyote and fox bait mini-farm that is much of American boredom satiation these crazy days.

So, we made our mutual non-aggression pact and were content to ignore one another for the most part after several of my recent afternoon strolls past their territory. I silently thanked them for their egg laying, and respected their boundaries (social and physical) by not coming any closer than the brick sidewalk would allow. Ever. For any reason.

It was a comfortable peace, albeit noisy from time to time.

On this balmy October Sunday eve — the peace was shattered.

11

FREEDOMMMMMMMM!

I began my Sunday sauntering much like any other adventure — rather routinely and blissfully unaware that barriers were compromised, and frontiers had been conquered. Strolling along without a thought of anything amiss, I was suddenly struck with the sight of a prison break. No alarms had been sounded, no mention of parole, but soon enough, I was… surrounded.

Growing up in the Midwestern United States has afforded me many such opportunities in the past to acquaint myself with these… curious creatures. I had heard tales of stubborn roosters and chicken coop raids that would make human toes curl, but even as a boy, I was never truly and properly introduced to these birds. I had been called their name and used it to mock others who displayed a lack of fortitude in the past, but suddenly I was thrust into a learning environment that was about to teach me about the true meaning of bravery.

They did not cower. They did not flinch. As I approached them, clearly on my side of the previously treatised boundary, they instead charged at my shorts-donned pale, exposed legs and flip-flopped feet. My bright white vulnerabilities were strikingly glaring in the sweltering afternoon sun.

I contacted the Lady of the House for guidance/instruction/protection. "Are the chickie-bock-bock's supposed to be out and following me like lost pups or…?" I texted her.

No immediate reply and none whatsoever it would turn out, but still my heart raced, and my sweat beads fell like raindrops at our feet.

Why was I nervous? Yes, I had chicken for lunch today. Yes, I'd had chicken for several lunches in my lifetime. And dinner. And probably even for breakfast. YES! And eggs! An incalculable mountain of eggs in countless meals and food and treats and holidays and desserts in the form of deviled eggs, cakes, frozen custard - all manner of chicken murder in my nearly half century on this planet.

Surely, we could let bygones be bygones in this tense standoff, willpower, dominance, or peace treaty violation, right?

Right?!

Enter: The Enforcers

It was clear to me now, that I was on the defensive and staging a somewhat saber-rattling retreat. There. I said it. The trio of Enforcers made it clear to me that, despite our previously enjoyed peace and relative respect, the rules had changed this afternoon and that in spite of their own newfound freedom I was to remain on the previously agreed-upon boundary of brick sidewalk and to venture no further. To ensure my compliance the three beaked bruisers surrounded me and stalked ever closer to my towering, somewhat quaking white towers of hairy middle-aged human man stilts.

Remembering my spent/wasted childhood and adolescence of video game adventures, I wiped the sweat from my brow, assessed the tactical situation, and then proved my courage by reaching out to my cousin to save me again.

"That's three of the four lost little cluckers following me and gossiping amongst themselves about my sweaty Star Wars t-shirt and sandals and shorts Sunday afternoon attire." I even sent her photographic reconnaissance proof of the standoff. To no avail. There was no reply.

"Five now. Five drumstick toters curiously eyeing me like I'm supposed to know where we're going and when we'll get there."

I could only imagine her strained sympathies as she was driving along the interstate, negotiating the dramas and nightmares and harrowing death-defying stunts required to navigate and survive the driving experience that is major U.S. metropolitan city traffic in the 21st Century. Regardless of the lady's silence, I continued my nervous and carefully monitored sidewalk movements, idiotic texting increasing alongside my confusion and nervousness. I had spotted more activity to the rear of their territory, where more winged avengers were waiting and making their agitation known.

"3 more darker broilers on the loose behind the pine trees, and the ducks are none too happy. I think they sense something fowl is afoot…"

No response.

"They are hurling insults at the freedom fowl. 'You're anything but quack-tastic!' and so on and so forth."

No reply.

In a bold move of brazen power boasting, The Enforcers shuttled me to a sunny spot on the sidewalk and laid down. I was stunned. I was dumbfounded. They were so cocksure of their flocky might that they actually had the nerve to sunbathe?!

Move along - nothing to see here!

I was so utterly shocked I nearly forgot my mouth was hanging open until the scent of their other yard wandering and territory-marking on the wind caught my nose and I covered it with my hand. I used the other one to make yet another plea to my kin, my protector, my ghoster.

"For their part, the tanner members of the Kentucky Colonel's wayward colony seem content to work on their tans…"

I'd reached a point of sweat and agitation and grump that I was losing control of my mental filters. Hearing no reply to my repeated signal flares, I finally lamented.

"Look, it's not my yard but I'm not afraid to tell you — loose peckers can do some serious damage unchecked."

Still not a peep. Except from the hens. These she-devils were mocking me in my own kin's yard, their home, their kingdom, their rules. I had had enough.

"THE LINE MUST BE DRAWN HERE!" I quoted my favorite Starfleet Captain and charged headlong into the fray. Soon I had rampage-stomped and flying-pig-arm-waved around the yard enough to pique their curiosity, and The Enforcers were none too happy about my peace treaty violation. The triplets rose from their leisurely sunbathing and began their proud march towards me. But I wouldn't have it. I am well north of two hundred pounds of Irish American brutality and I will not be bullied. By anyone or anything. Ever. Again.

Peck.

"GAH!!! NO! STOP IT!"

Peck...peck...PECK!

"FOR THE LOVE OF… OWW! KNOCK IT OFF, YOU LITTLE…"

Peck peck peck, peck PECK PECK…**PECK!**

Like I mentioned at the beginning of this operational debrief, this experience was a learning opportunity. Part of what I learned is that chicken beaks are made of titanium and diamonds. And, when thrust at exposed manflesh that are my pasty legs with lightning quickness? There is very little you can do about it except move. Out of range. If you're not surrounded.

I began my undulating drunk ninja bunny hop maneuver with rapid expediency and extricated myself from the field of fire, much to the confusion and chagrin of the gang of feathered thugs. How something so large and loud and…sweaty could move so fast was beyond their schemes and only their hateful glares were attacking me now. I rubbed and slapped my throbbing shins and noticed as I applied my imaginary healing salve the sound seemed to startle my foes. Not only startle but encourage them to… retreat?!

EUREKA! THE DAY IS MINE! Here comes the sweaty clappy-clap monster, here to corral the gizzard chorale and RECLAIM THE BRICKS AS HOLY GROUND!

"BACK! BACK YOU DEVILS!" I lambasted the future nugget baskets, channeling my inner Samwise Gamgee (see: Lord of the Rings).

One of the egg droppers clucked and protested her way back into her coop with only a couple of sonic assaults. Soon another was similarly motivated. And… next… AN ENFORCER! She's in!

You…shall not ..PASS!

I wasted no time in slamming the door and "HA-HA!!" bullhorning my triumphant victory to an audience of, well, no one in the surrounding yard space. Far from a hollow victory, I decided to update the homeowner on the ongoing drama.

"Eureka! Three apprehended! The other two are more… serious… and not so… cooperative. This is why I fix computers and am not a farmer."

Much to my dismay the remaining two jailbirds were making a break for the open range. I desperately signaled again.

"Now two of the tanners are joining their darker meat friends on the other side of the pines. It's nugget stampede pandemonium!"

How was I going to catch them? I was convinced they would be found by someone or some… THING else far quicker than I could catch them. As I looked frustrated at the escaping future feather pillows, a glimmer of hope arrived. It seemed my carrier pigeon text messages had indeed been received, because at that pivotal moment the Lord of the House sent up a signal flare of his own.

"I let the chickens out to eat some stink bugs," he texted.

I was simultaneously relieved and exasperated. Apparently temporary parole/pest control exercises were the norm in this kingdom. I had accomplished nothing but interfering with a controlled extermination effort.

My foes were not impressed with my performance. In a final act of clucking defiance, they made their way up the gangway into the adjoining coop, pecked their way out the unlocked door, and flappily descended their way back into the grub and bug-rich grass buffet.

I felt smarter somehow. Vindicated. My lesson had cost me blood, sweat, and even a few tears. But they were tears of laughter. How many idiots does it take to figure out a wild goose chase involving Mafioso chicken future cutlet treats might just be safer observed from the safety of a kitchen window? Apparently more than just *this one*.

Moral of the story: leave plucky chickens alone. Don't trust their calls of friendship and innocence. And enjoy every single bite of chicken you take for the rest of your life because… YOU'VE EARNED IT AND THEY DESERVE IT!

Now if you'll excuse me… I believe buffalo wings may be on the dinner menu tonight.

COVID BIRDS

This morning started normally. As "normal" as the present definition can be found.

Cheerios and The Today Show.

Social distancing.

Death, disease, and dreadful news.

Teaspoon after teaspoon of soggy cereal with a side of human suffering.

Puppy at my feet, cats pawing at the patio door to be let out into the treacherous world beyond.

And then it happened.

A gorgeous male Cardinal so scorching red it made me hold my breath.

Yes, the accompanying gasp caused a minor milky Cheerio explosion as I choked and coughed my way gracefully to another mess to be cleaned up, but after...

The TV went off.

The silence descended.

Peace.

A Mourning Dove pair next. "What now, Misses?" "Over here, Sir." "No, nothing doing here. How about over yonder?"

A Robin. Bounce. Bounce. BOUNCE! Then another.

Sparrow 1.. Sparrow 2... Sparrows 11, 12, and 13.

A Red-winged Blackbird strikes in.

A Starling. Head side-to-side, shimmering.

Purple Finch.

A bully Blue Jay causes some commotion; kitteh eyes widen and they chitter.

The dance. The ballet. The flit and flight of wing and cheep. Cheep-cheep.

Unabashed sunflower seed massacre.

And then something else happened.

RED-TAILED HAWK!

The swoop was startling to me, but worse for the seed seekers.

No warning, no hint of paradise lost... just... BOOM!

Absolute pandemonium as every color exploded in instant furious feathery exodus!

Bird feeders swinging. Cats are never more grateful to be indoors. Furry critters indoors and feathered critters outdoors scattering in every direction.

The red-tail landed on the fence facing the feeders.

Most awesome coloring adorning such a lethal predator.

I held my breath, gazing at him in wonder. I slipper-shuffled to the door, pulled in by his beauty.

The sharpness of his glare.

His head snapping this direction and that, calculating what went wrong; midnight black razor sharp claws finding only fence wood this morning.

Our eyes met.

His impression of me... nonchalant. Too big for prey, coated in soggy cereal spit-up.

Epic calculation skills indeed.

A deep breath from Mr. Judgey Hawk Claws of Aerial Murder, and his launch was almost as impressive as his landing.

Enormous wings carrying evolutionary death on the wing into hopefully more fruitful hunting grounds.

Calm returns.

The chilly breeze.

Puppy staring out the door with me. Why is Dad staring at nothing and why is he dripping soggy tasty bits?

The songbirds returned slowly one by one.

Mourning doves goose-necking around, surveying the damage. "Still nothing, Missus." "Over here, Mister..."

Robins' "Roundaleeee!" chorus interrupted only by their hop-hop worm hunting adventures. Boing. BOING!

A pair of cardinals this time; the male as striking as ever. The female eats first.

The brown horde sparrow army advancing en masse.

A blue jay shrieking shame from the same fence the real threat just launched from. His blowhard braggadocio all for naught.

A deep breath from me, grateful for this morning's lesson:

Find your peace.

It's out there.

It may be interrupted from time to time.

But it's always worth the hunt.

A WIZARD ARRIVES PRECISELY

Gandalf, my cat, likes to make an entrance.

He remains out of sight until he is ready for you to know of his presence, and thereby remind the pesky human(s) of his magnificent majesty over you. His lordship will wander the baseboards, rubbing and purring and merrrrowing at all levels. And then he spots his victim/servant...

The squishy manbag that is the procurer of kibble.

The deliverer of deliciousness.

The peeler of peel-top cans.

He makes his approach deliberate, and announces his displeasure with your obvious lack of delectable delivery within the last five minutes with a solid:

"MRRRRRRRRRROW!"

If this grabs your attention and you motivate your bones to try to pet him, he's got you. The lure is set and your lip is hopelessly hooked.

A step away. "Mrrreow?"

Another step as you fruitlessly attempt to reach and console his cat-jesty.

A quick trot and he's opened up a gap that allows him to flop down and rub his face scritchy-scratchy super cutely on the carpet with purrs and trills and irresistible adorableness.

You giggle with glee and attempt the pets and toe bean touches and you prance excruciatingly close, and your hand barely graces the softest fur your feeble human brain could ever imagine and this makes your crack kitty addiction enflamed to insane levels of withdrawal like the most addictive substance in nature and...

Like a flash he's up like a spring and bounding towards the ultimate destination and focus of his disdain:

A food bowl filled so full of food it points like an inverted funnel to the very bare center which gleams like a silver dollar in blinding brilliance as a center of nothingness.

His Lordship continues to rub and purrs and merrowwwwws against anything AROUND the crime scene EXCLUDING your own leg as he looks at the food bowl.

And then back to you.

And then back to the food bowl.

And then back to you.

And then back to the food bowl.

You glance towards the bag of dry cat food.

EUREKA! The human can be trained!

The moment you acknowledge the "problem" and your ability to "solve" it is the moment his superiority is justified.

I am a 41-year-old American man, and this seven pound sauntering ego of tooth and claw and fur has reduced me to a kibble vending machine.

If I try to explain the ludicrous nature of his request? Or worse... meander my way away from the unmitigated disaster?

"MROW!"

The King is displeased. Obviously, you didn't get the message.

He blocks your retreat. He narrows his eyes. He corrals you back in salvation's direction.

If you manage to step over the spry little grey feline speed bump?

Not so fast! He's on you like a flash.

He negotiates once more.

"MRRRRRROOOOWWWW!"

"Right merrrrow?" you ask.

A whisker-wind of a hufflepuff semi-sneeze of indignation comes from the royalty as he stomps off, leaving a dismissive cloud of furry annoyance in his wake.

You might stand and wonder how so much attitude got packed into one tiny little fuzzball, but...

Might I offer this as evidence of a higher power at work?

I just never guessed it was a feline deity we are all here to serve.

Maybe the Egyptians and their tomb pictures were right all along!

Life is so much better with a cat that our ultimate tribute to them is taking them with us all the way to the grave and the great beyond.

THE SNEEZE

B-dubs. Lunch. Excellence in breaded boneless chicken Nirvana. Trivia on tablets. Music videos. Sports channels. Good service with warm smiles. Sunshine, inside and out, pretty much the perfect break for the day. My wondrous church o'chicken!

And then it happened.

I could feel it coming.

There was nothing I could do to stop it...

I instinctively reached for my napkin, wadded and saucy though it may be. My shield. My savior. My... trampoline.

My mother has the loudest sneeze in recorded human history. I'm pretty sure she borrowed the sound of the cataclysmic explosion the meteor made when it nerfed the dinos into extinction. When she sneezes inside a car with the windows up? Has anyone seen that movie "Snatch" when a would-be robber tries out a pistol full of blank bullets inside the getaway car with the windows up? Yeah, windows shatter and they all go deaf. It's exactly like that - only without the dog and three black guys getting ready to rob an unhinged mobster bookie.

31

Unlike my mother I was "encouraged" to temper my sneezes growing up. Who could blame my father for trying to steer clear of yet another nuclear blast of mucosal malaise from yet another sinus-cursed member of his family? So, in all fairness to my friends, family, and the general public, up until recently I was even able to hold my sneezes in.

But not today!

Today was a reckoning. Today was a lesson in self-awareness. Today was...a natural disaster.

Not only was I trying to contain the sneeze, but I was also trying to do it with a mouthful of the healthiest thing I usually ever eat - a mouthful of carrots. And we're not talking about the first few timid nibbles of veggie delight - we're talking about a cauldron of burbly-bubbly blue-cheesey concoction of itty-bitty carrot-ite muck-fetti.

The explosion was brutal. Thank GOD my eyes squint shut when I sneeze. When they opened? It was like all the world was orange marmalade. How it didn't rain down on the tables surrounding us is a modern-day miracle. I was covered. It was on my shirt, on the table, in my iced tea, all over the floor... it had blizzarded B-Dubs with carrot-ling snow while I closed my eyes and feared the inevitable blast.

I'm pretty sure the county health department would fail the place if they knew what just happened. Much to my lunch companions' credit, if some carrot precipitation had befallen their drinks or food they either didn't notice or didn't care.

I sheepishly cleaned up as much of my mess as I could without a HAZMAT suit, paid my bill, and made my way out of the restaurant with as much dignity as I could muster:

None.

HEARTLAND HEARTBREAK

By the numbers:

Tom Petty and the Heartbreakers - 40th Anniversary Tour
Indianapolis, IN - Saturday, May 13th, 2017
8:00 pm EST

Otherwise known as the last concert at Deer Creek/Verizon/
Klipsch/Ruoff Home Mortgage Music Center I will ever attend.

20 minutes to make it into the venue after the commute, parking, and
walking up to the gate. Security screening after standing shoulder to
shoulder and breathing down the necks of fellow anxious
concertgoers.

20 minutes to buy a forty-five-dollar t-shirt celebrating one of the
greatest rock bands of all time. At least they took credit cards.

20 minutes in line for the first round of porta-potty putridity.

20 minutes of walking, hiking, hurrying, scurrying, bumping,
bruising, pushing, pulling, rushing, shuffling, slipping, sliding,
slinking, outright shoving our way past, beside, inside, outside,
around, under, over, and through thousands of people to find two

friends amidst an undulating, agitated sea of humanity.

20 lungfuls of secondhand marijuana and cigarette smoke. This would be the prevailing air quality for the entire march.

20 female boobs accidentally brushed/smashed/hugged/touched during the hellacious hike.

1.5 songs heard from opener Joe Walsh = "Life's Been Good" and "Rocky Mountain Way."

9:10 pm = friends located; I head for my own porta-potty relief.

3 hours later will be the next time I see my friends.

9:15 pm = Tom Petty takes the stage.

9:25 pm = I use the porta-potty for the only time all evening, but not before the line endures a verbal tirade by a large drunken woman for taking too long to move along. The first line we stood in for the same reason earlier was similarly lectured by a younger but equally drunken woman.

It was at this point in the evening I had a moment of clarity. I stared up into the swarm of hops and barley worshippers on the lawn, wiped the sweat from my brow, and considered my options. A light breeze kicked up, the food carnival area was still full of people, but nothing like the gawking, cawing mass that was that lawn. I decided reliving my first anxiety attack while swimming in sweaty human dancing excrement wasn't worth it.

I found a safe space. I could hear the music. The breeze was heavenly relief. I opened my water bottle for the first time and drank it all. I was rewarded for my decision by half a dozen people (men AND women) urinating in the pine trees behind me.

I found another safe space. I was back near the front gate, very few people. I could still hear the music. I could still feel the breeze. I bought an eight-dollar bottle of water. I observed a drunken couple arguing, wandering around, then finally standing still. The argument intensifies. The man drops his thirteen-dollar Coors Light and cigarette and unloads an absolute haymaker on the woman's jaw. The sound her skull makes when she hits the concrete sounds like a dropped bowling ball. She's not moving. Security and a cop tackle him. Ambulance called; she's moving now but only because her stretcher has wheels. I remain in my safe space, note the irony of "You Don't Know How It Feels" wafting on the air in the background.

10:00 pm and I've lost count of how many drunks I've seen this night. I've seen a man snorting cocaine. I smell cigarette and marijuana smoke everywhere. Then the vomiting exhibitions begin. One twenty-something woman begins the chunky liquid coughing, and it suddenly turns into a deluge of Coors-sponsored grass watering. Her beefcake date looks on nervously, I turn away and drink my water. Sometime later a woman sits in the wet spot and curses life as she swipes at her new derpmuck moistened shorts and bare legs.

A party of young trustees of modern chemistry soon sits beside me in my safe spot. I wisely scoot down. The quartet is in rough shape, obviously drunk, obviously lost, still sucking face and carrying on with copious groping. The two "men" are laughing and cursing about a limo when one of their dates empties her stomach contents onto the grass behind us, the males laughing at her and giving no shits. One of the guys lights a cigarette, gives her a drag of it and a swig of beer, then continues making out with her. Derp smooches with raging tongue action!

I've seen enough. I'm out of Klipsch, never to return.

I lean on the rear truck bumper, finally alone. Cool breeze, music still discernible. Finally at peace.

Not so fast...

Trickling out of the venue behind me are the other early birds. Along with their fleeing instincts they also bring with them full bladders. More public urination. Both sexes. I put on my concert t-shirt; it's black and should help me further blend into the shadows. More music, more drunks... I will be hiding on the bumper for almost two more hours.

Around midnight the concert finally mercifully ends. But the show isn't over. The party continues when the drunks all find automobiles to drive. One of them in a white Nissan SUV decides to attempt ninja stealth mode and charges headlong into the field behind our parking lot to avoid the insane exit waiting lines. What the genius finds instead is a fence. Smashes into it. Turns around. Headlights on, beaming back at me. Finally, the manner of my death is revealed to me. No more questions. No more waiting. Here it comes. See you soon, Grandpa. Instead of killing me he swerves onto the gravel path at the last moment, over-corrects, mounts an Earthen berm and continues his off-roading adventures elsewhere.

Friends made it back to the truck safely. We made it home around 2:30 am. I hugged them and said my goodbyes.

But I forgot one.

Goodbye, Deer Creek/Verizon/Klipsch/Ruoff Home Mortgage whateverland. Thank you for Mumford & Sons, Brad Paisley, Collective Soul, Reba McIntyre, and my first concert ever: Paula Abdul on my thirteenth birthday. And thank you for making the decision to never return an easy one. I just don't have the heart for your grotesquery anymore. Or the stomach.

37

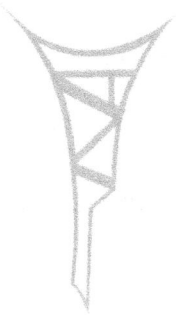

PICKUP THE FLAG

I saw a pickup truck today that had the confederate battle flag decal (I use "battle" in the description because the true confederate flag is the white one of surrender), a "Don't Tread on Me" decal, a Thin Blue Line decal, and a US Marines decal on his back window.

None of these stickers strike me as especially offensive or controversial on their own, but I'm aware that opinions vary of who's offended and why in 21st century America. But aren't some of these icons of freedom somewhat... contradictory?

The confederate states preached freedom while enslaving an entire race for unchecked free-market financial gain. The Civil War corrected this behavior in America for all time and at a terrible cost on both sides. But okay, carry on, Confederate son...

The Don't Tread on Me flag was originally created during the Revolutionary War when America fought for its freedom to self-govern and free itself from British rule. Again, at a terrible cost in human lives. But okay, fly it as some symbol of patriotism and freedom in 2020...

The Thin Blue Line is a silver-and-black American flag with a single stripe colored blue. This is meant to display support for American police men and women, who are charged with serving and protecting American civilians. They are often responsible for saving and protecting lives from people who misinterpret the American concept of freedom to mean they can behave however they want whenever they want without consequence. They are often harassed and even outright attacked for doing thankless jobs with unsuitable or aging equipment against criminals better equipped and unburdened with thoughts of the rule of law. This sticker is meant to be flown in support of those who protect freedom by enforcing the laws written to protect us all. But why is it flanked by the other three? Odd.

Finally, the US Marines decal, in concert with the US Marines veteran license plate, is a proud placard of declared dedication/service to the United States Marines Corps, a celebrated, powerful, feared branch of the United States Military, who are also tasked with protecting America on or from foreign shores. This is a simple sign of membership or support of the Marines. Okay, fair enough. Least controversial of all.

So why fly all four stickers on the same rolling billboard? I can only assume they're meant to display an attitude of pride, patriotism, and service to your fellow countrymen...? Or a rolling raised fist of defiance towards anyone and everyone who would take away your freedom(s)? Or the different colors made a beautiful mix of rainbow brilliance, and your attitude of gay rights should be equally championed and protected like every other American freedom is best served abstractly on your truck's back window for all to see?

Flying the confederate flag today anywhere at all in America is a huge controversy, so I guess this is the one that most makes the rest tempted to pull a corner loose and let the wind carry them to loftier display... maybe that's the point? To mix confusion and racism with patriotism and freedom and call it a political party?

39

Or... maybe they're just stickers? And they make the owner happy so that's why they're there?

HOMEOWNERSHIP
AND THE AMERICAN DREAM

Last year I became a homeowner for the first time in my life.

The American Dream.

The pinnacle of freedom.

The ultimate reward for employment, paying taxes, following reasonable personal economic policies, and obeying federal, state, or local laws.

A place where I can wash my socks and undies without waiting for someone else's laundry to be done.

A place where I can park my car in my own driveway and/or garage day and night without wishing, hoping, or praying I don't discover someone else in my spot.

A place where I can use the restroom whenever I want for as long as I want and for whatever I want. I'll skip waxing poetic on these activities any further.

A place where I can keep my Christmas tree up until the end of

January because it suits me, and I hearts it.

A place where I can turn the volume on my TV, computer, or speakers up or down to my heart's content anywhere between AC/DC Thunderstruck 1987 at Madison Square Garden and Enya Watermark in an elevator at the Waldorf Astoria on early Sunday mornings.

A place where I can set the thermostat to sub-arctic or Kīlauea volcano according to my bare toe temps and sweat gland protests.

A place where I can tend my lawn however I see fit. And can build a fence around it. Or kill all my grass because green is so 1980's and 2020-21 brown is a much more Covid saga-summarizing color.

Oops. Forgot about one little snag.

The HOA.

This modern interpretation of the Nazi politick has the unmitigated gall to charge me $XX.XX per month to enforce policies and standards that modern Americans have to be told are good ideas to maintain increased or stable home values and theoretically improved neighborly relationships for everyone foolish enough to submit to the requirements of HOA membership to own a home in the neighborhood. "If everyone will just follow the rules and play nice, we will all get along!" And heeeeeeere we go!

For example, good HOA ideas or covenants such as no backyard fences on pond lots. Why? It's a retention pond, and fences prevent larger vehicles like fire trucks from getting to them in emergency retention pond situations such as drowning by prohibited fishing, skating, or swimming activities engaged by foolhardy hard-headed human types. Except my "pond lot" is actually one enormous utility easement away from being an actual pond lot, so when my home builder offered to build me a backyard privacy fence for the cost of my home, I declined the offer because of a mammoth forty-page HOA covenant encyclopedia Titanicca that told me I couldn't have one. Except it turns out I could. And every house on this row except mine and one other found out, too, so they have fences. The cost of the fence and its labor wasn't deducted from my mortgage by a single cent. But I digress...

Good HOA ideas and covenants such as exterior color choices and changes must be cleared by the HOA prior to making them. To my own home. Like flying an American flag. Political yard signs are forbidden. And no spotlights/bonfires/animal sacrifices anywhere in my yard. But I still hung my gorgeous Jedi Master wreath on the front door because I have every idea a Jedi Mind Trick will be infinitely powerful compared to anyone who dares tread on my property to challenge its placement, color, size, scent, etc. I get it that ritualistic animal slaughter may be offensive to those with weaker constitutions, but... this isn't the wreath you're looking for... (finger waggle)

Good HOA ideas and covenants such as no derelict vehicles parked on the streets. No rebuilding engines in driveways that cause fluid leaks and groundwater contamination and pollution of all kinds. Except my neighbor can idle his 1982 Chevy POS Hoonigan lowrider Silverado for 45 minutes this morning in his driveway (as he does every morning) and his illegal catalytic converter-less and muffler-less exhaust has now filled my home with a toxic stench that's making my lungs and nostrils burn, my eyes water, my stomach wretch, and my repeated pleas for law enforcement... enforcement to go unanswered.

Good HOA ideas and covenants like sidewalks and street lamps for residents and guests to feel safe whilst jogging at night, or taking a leisurely stroll to enjoy the splendor of mother nature, or to walk up my driveway and into my front yard to traipse around at their heart's content so Rover the Chow/Shepherd mix can take enormous dumps wherever he wants and you can smear it across my sod as you hastily wipe it into a leaky plastic bag. Twice. In less than a week.

Good HOA ideas and covenants like spending $XX.XX/month will ensure your fellow trespassers, polluters, and law breakers can do as they please without fear of reprisal, as long as they don't paint their house Hot Pink with Chartreuse flower pots in brown mulch without submitting their plans to the HOA Hauspolizei first in triplicate, pay an additional fee in singed nose hairs and dog dew smeared grass clippings, and wait six to twenty-four months for a decision to do what they want with their "own" property.

Oh, and for all of my official questions/comments/concerns submitted to the HOA in my six months of homeownership?

"Unfortunately, the HOA does not get involved or handle any domestic situations. We would hope you'd agree that it's not a good use of the police resources to mitigate situations like this. Everyone is new in the HOA, and we would suggest being a good neighbor, and try to have a conversation with the other person and come to an amicable resolution. If not, you may have to resign yourself to the fact that some people are just not responsible pet owners, neighbors, and human beings."

I want my HOA fees back. I wonder what their response to that would be… an eviction notice? I wonder if that would take six to twenty-four months, too...

Now if you'll excuse me, I'll return to my antacids and nose sprays and house fumigation and watching my driveway like a hawk for a police cruiser that has yet to appear hours after it was first summoned.

FURNITURE DELIVERY

Last July, I bought my very first home thanks - in no small part - to the help, guidance, and patience of my friend and realtor, Jennifer. Not long after moving in, I decided to upgrade my seating capacity from two fine garage sale purchases my mother made to a large sectional couch that fills the room. Just in case a wandering tribe of gypsies stops by, or family, or friends, they'll all have a place to sit besides the sea of dark grey, plushy velvet, cat-claw-sharpening softness that is my new carpet.

A friend of mine who lives in this neighborhood had the most comfortable couch I'd ever sat on in the perfect color, and he told me he acquired it from Bob's Discount Furniture in Indianapolis. So, I made a call. I ordered the sofa with all the options, and the sales lady scoffed at me when I asked how long the delivery would take.

"Well, your website told me two weeks..." I sheepishly replied.

"Honey, it's COVID. America is stuck at home. Do you really think you're getting this enormous seven-piece sectional in two weeks? You'll be lucky to have it in seven weeks!"

Great. At least I got the special financing along with all the special treatment. I signed up for standard delivery and sat in one of two chairs for the next two months.

Seven weeks to the day later, on September 4, I was standing in my brand-new home anxiously awaiting my shiny new heiny tarmac. The XPO Logistics Delivery drivers arrived and asked me to open my garage door. I asked them politely to deliver my enormous couch pieces inside my front door instead, as such a service was offered at the time of my purchase. I did not opt for the upgraded delivery service because it was twice the price, and I could surely unwrap and set up a titanic sectional sofa all by myself.

(#dowork #geterdone #manskillz)

Frowny faces notwithstanding, they complied with my unreasonable request. Everything was fine until...

Deliveryman #1: "Wait, hold up!"

Delivery Man #2: "I got this..."

Delivery Man #1: "No, wait a minute!"

Delivery Man #2: "STAND BACK! I GOT THIS MF'ER!"

The wedged sofa section plugging my front door hole came exploding into my entryway with the force of an Indianapolis Colts legend Dwight Freeny blitz, and along with the sound of a sickening door frame wood crack came Deliveryman #2's triumphant, vulgar exclamation of his allusional panicular girth:

"Sometimes you gots to just smash that hole even if your package don't quite fit! PUSH HARDER, SHE'LL GIVE IN!"

I looked at Delivery Man #1.

I looked at Delivery Man #2.

I looked at my door.

I looked at my floor.

Door seemed fine.

Vinyl floor was scraped all the way down to the concrete foundation in several places.

Delivery Man #1: "... oops?" he grinned at me.

Delivery Man #2: "Well, that's what you get for ordering the cheap delivery. If you would've paid for the upgraded delivery, this wouldn't have happened!"

They then proceeded to drag the furniture to my living room carpet, leaving further damage on my vinyl floor in the form of furrows the size of cornrows to the carpet line.

I thanked them for their "service," and told them I could take it from here.

No apologies.

No contact information on who to call about the damage.

As they were leaving, I asked Delivery Man #1 (the least poetic of the duet) who I should contact about the damage.

"Gee, that's a tough call there, bud. I'm not sure..." he trailed off as they hurried away back to their truck and tore out of the neighborhood.

I immediately called Bob's Discount Furniture and waited on hold for four hours and got disconnected.

Alright, at least the sofa was in the house, and I could set it up. It was unharmed and beautiful and exactly what I wanted.

I called Bob's Discount Furniture on Monday. Another four hours on hold and disconnected. So, being the savvy I.T. guy that I am, I went online and filled out a contact form for customer service.

A week later after hearing nothing, I sent another email.

Two days later I called back. I actually spoke with a human after waiting on hold for two hours. Email address obtained, I sent pictures of the damage that I took immediately after the incident.

Did you ever see the movie "Cast Away" with Tom Hanks? That part where he's been on the island for a few days or weeks and then the scene fades out and comes back after another round of time has passed, only this block of time revelation made you gasp?

Five and a half months later, I got a check in the mail for the damage. But I had to send 2-3 emails a week, every week, even on Christmas Eve, asking, begging, politely cautioning I was prepared to file a small claims lawsuit against XPO and Bob's. Phone calls. More emails. More phone calls.

Silence. Excuses. This person here, that person there. Someone's dog died. Someone was on vacation. Someone was having an ingrown toenail removed. Someone was learning Swahili, and the Kraft Macaroni and Cheese box translation in Abu Dhabi Arabic was giving them all manner of frustration just trying to cook Kraft dinner for the kiddos and oh Covid and what was your name and case number again and but the warehouse manager in Chicago handles these and what store did you buy this from and didn't the warehouse manager in Chicago handle this yet and... who are you?

Over seven months and $300 later, my floor was fixed by two amazingly professional installers who, probably like anyone who's still reading at this point, were left with their jaws wide open like Pearl Jam's Jeremy after hearing this tale of my Irish luck.

And I still have the customer satisfaction survey to fill out!

Part Two: Remembering

Speaking of rose-colored glasses, I find them no harder to shuck than when trying to patiently, honestly, and innocently inspect the Past.

I've had many discussions with countless male family members and friends through the years and have found their stories to be more about the events and things of life; the female members of my sphere tend to remember more about the people and places when it comes to memory. I cannot fault a single member of either group because my own memory limitations make several wholly worthy events all but invisible, while the most useless, random, seemingly worthless knowledge can make me a ringer at almost any Trivia pursuit.

Those territories of my mind that find themselves peppered with the glint of fading memory are some of my favorite places to explore. I try not to dwell in them too long; I remind myself that for all the space the Past and Future may take up in my thoughts, the Present is fleeting but just as sacred.

Here are some works devoted to remembrance, and the pursuit of it without the heavy fog of distortive nostalgia whenever possible.

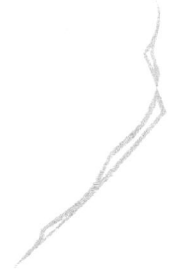

GRANDPARENTS

When I was a boy, there was no greater joy than the event that was walking into my grandparents' house.

A two-story gray house with a maroon roof in little Dayton, Indiana, it was built at the turn of the twentieth century by my great-great-grandfather, aptly surnamed Carpenter. The feeling I got when I squeezed the front door handle, twisted, and pushed open the heavy oak door was always near elation. Soon, I would be pelted by falling folded newspaper bits that my grandfather stuffed into the door seal because it did anything but that, and, thus, the dusty, inky baptism commenced as my entrance continued. Further in I would confidently stride, knowing the person or people I sought loved me more than life itself - there was nothing to fear here. The smell of coffee wafting in from the kitchen, sometimes the sounds of the Chicago Cubs on the ancient AM/FM radio, or the Weather Channel on the RCA TV that didn't even have a remote control. Over the pea-green carpet decades older than I was, I would move into the TV Room.

And there, sitting on an old, green "davenport," I would visit with the two people I find I miss more than most these days - my Grandma Rosemary and Grandpa Gaylord. Grandma playing Solitaire with a deck of cards so worn the suits were almost completely gone from their corners, Grandpa reading the newspaper or gazing out the window down Washington Street outside.

Oh, how I miss those people! Oh, how I miss that love! Oh, how I miss that WISDOM!

Grandma: "Nicholas, your mother told me about your report card. That's not fair. You have a gift; you're smarter than that. Other children have to work twice as hard to get half the grades you do. You can do better." These lessons always followed a hug, and never harsh.

Grandpa: "Nick, the green light on the VCR is flashing again. Can you help me fix it?" I leapt at the chance to help my living hero.

Grandma: "There's a box of Nilla Wafers in the pantry - go get those and bring them to Grandma." She knew I always sneaked two for myself on the return trip (the real secret was she didn't ask for them for herself).

Grandpa: "Nick, let's go out and burn some of those leaves." Some of my most cherished memories in life are the conversations I had with Grandpa during those countless outdoor projects.

Grandma: "Don't you listen to Grandpa! You eat that piece of cheese." Grandma didn't care if I was fat - she loved me anyway.

Grandpa: "Nicholas Michael, don't you ever start smoking. Those cigarettes are nothing but little white lies and they're not the same as when I was your age. They're full of poison now..." I started smoking in March of 2001 and it took me another thirteen years to conquer it. Grandpa never had one with me, but he knew I smoked and asked to sniff an unlit cigarette from time to time.

Grandma: "Nicholas, you and Timothy (my brother) have to help us with Communion at church on Sunday, so come find us after the service." Faith. Always faith. Both of my grandparents were overflowing with it.

Grandpa: "Nicholas, one time you were singing 'Jesus Loves Me' when you were little and I asked you "well, what about Grandpa?" and the next verse you sang "Jesus loves Grandpa!" He cackled like he was being tickled by a feather.

It is my most sincere wish that someone loves you the way my Grandma and Grandpa loved me, and you love them back as fiercely as you were blessed with it.

NO GOOD DEED

I make a lot of mistakes.

In fact, sometimes I feel like the only thing I get right about my humanity is making mistakes. But this morning? I saved a life.

I was pulling out of the garage to go to work, just another normal workday, looking forward to just another day of normalcy when life, fate, God, or nature made other plans. As I drove along the alleyway, I noticed something furiously arguing with a particularly annoying bush. This is the same bush that threatens the gorgeous paint job on my muscle car every day with its all-too-close-for-comfort limbs. Only this time it was threatening something else. The battle raged as I drove past, leaving to life, fate, God, or nature the outcome of the warfare and its ultimate cosmic significance.

But then this niggling little thought ninja wormed its way inside my brain and sliced and diced its way through my conscience.

"There had to be something I could do."

"Don't interfere - if God wants that life to continue, He'll save it."

"Yeah, but what if that 'doing' is supposed to be me?"

"My, my! Aren't we feeling high and mighty today?"

"No, but I might be able to help?"

"You'll be late for work!"

The angel and devil on opposite shoulders continued lobbing argument grenades at one another until I slammed on the brakes and turned around for home.

"This is insane! This is not your fight! ...But if I am able to do something and I don't do something then that makes me just... an asshole."

They continued arguing for control of me until I saw it.

I have a special place in my heart for Indiana's songbirds. My maternal grandmother was a notorious ornithologist wannabe, studying them intensely for years from her kitchen window during their daily feasts of seeds and suet in her backyard. She had a book older than her children she used to read to me with pictures and facts about many of her favorites; the dazzling Cardinal, the beautiful Purple Finch, the bully bastard Blue jays, the darling Goldfinch, the sweet but dwindling bluebird, the flashy Red-Winged blackbird. Here was my chance to save one. Not so celebrated as the handsome oriole, not so enormous as the Great Blue Heron, but a familiar yard-hopper nonetheless.

The enraged robin continued to furiously writhe and struggle and flap its wings and chirp and rage against its captor - a single branch of that bastard bush! I shut off the engine and stepped out of the car.

The phantom motivators began their chorus again.

"Oh dear, you can't help. A stray cat will come along soon and finish what God started...How in the world am I gonna help that thing when it's panicking and thrashing around like that? I could make it worse! ...Exactly. Get back in your car and go to work - there's nothing you can do."

And then I saw it: a string! Suddenly everything became clear! The tiniest of tiny white threads was threatening the entire life of this bird. It had become wrapped and furiously entangled around the bird's foot, binding it to the branch of that damned paint-job-threatening evil bush! No second-guessing, no more doubt.

The motivation chorus went silent and the bird shrieked and thrashed in unholy terror as I approached the battlefield with metallic vengeance in hand. In a flash the little white string was cut by my pocketknife, and the plump robin that had once risked its life for its ensnaring nest-building material was sitting on top of the neighbor's garage staring back at me. A beak strike at the leftover string wrapped around its foot, and all evidence of the vicious entanglement was gone once and for all.

The bird took off for loftier goals I can only assume, but not before reminding me of one of life's most important lessons.

A giant bird poop landed on my sunroof with a sickening **SPLAT!!**

It was so loud I flinched. The robin thanked me and made his opinion of my cherished muscle car known in one single bombs away hurray display of nature's greatest glory. I laughed at the irony like a mad man the entire way to work.

Thanks for the visit this morning, Grandma.

And yes, I remember. No good deed goes unpunished.

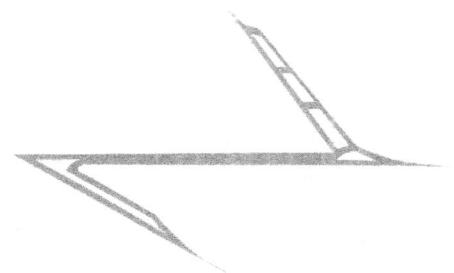

THE TASTE OF VICTORY

It was our first scrimmage against the eighth graders.

I was big for my age. Roly-poly mode managed since first grade when I took dead last in the Spring Fling foot races. I had swept all the blue ribbons just the year before in kindergarten. I looked big for my age. Felt big. Was big.

I was playing right guard on this football team. Coached by my math teacher, who I somewhat idolized as the ideal male. Beard. Smart-ass. Gruff. Gave me no leeway on the field or off. Immune to my usual bullshit. He once ran us so hard and so long during a Saturday practice I couldn't hold it any longer and soiled myself. Then, I had the honor of being discovered in the locker room showers washing out my practice pants so I could rejoin the team on the field. "The Glory Days" indeed.

Coach warned us about what was about to happen - the eighth grade was tough. Instructed to give no quarter. Show no mercy. Flashbacks to Karate Kid played in my mind. Yes, Mr. Myagi - crane kicks only for grandiose final battle maneuvers. Hairy knuckles wrapped around and tugging on my facemask with reality-returning warnings to behave likewise or expect... bleacher-bound, fully geared physical

57

"conditioning" the next day. Message received; message understood.

So, it began. The day was hot. Sunset blazing amber and heat waves roasting off shiny aluminum bleacher seats-slash-torture platforms. Sweat pouring off of us. Little water to keep us from drinking too much and "making ourselves sick."

"Swish it around and SPIT IT OUT!"

Defense put up little of it and the eighth graders made quick work of seven points and shrinking underclassmen school pride. Cheers and jeers from the sprinkling of onlookers. Team managers. Cheerleaders waiting for their rides. Siblings. Assistant coaches. Furious head coaches on both sides.

My name is called. Put up or shut up. Stomach in knots, incredible heat bearing down on my navy-blue jersey. What was I thinking? I was a church boy, a choir boy, a band geek, a computer nerd - anything but an athlete. What the hell was I doing trotting onto this field?

"MOVE YOUR ASS, JUMBO!" - Coach's encouragement to find another gear. Oh, right. Need to focus. Head in the game. Job to do. Protect the quarterback. Fill a hole. Right.

In strode Chris from the opposing sideline, somewhat gracefully. Tall. Like a ladder to climb trees. Seemingly unaffected by the sweltering heat. The guy that ran with the rougher crowd but seemed nicer than most of them. Always wore raggy Metallica t-shirts during school. Quick to laugh. Lined up across from me. Nothing to worry about; he'd always ignored me in the hallways and never made a single aggressive comment or even flinch towards me, I outweighed him by at least twenty pounds...

Suddenly... grass. I know that smell. What is that sound? It's something sliding on it. Plastic. Hard. Helmet! A helmet sliding on grass. The echo of a shattering impact and lungs on fire as hot as the four o'clock sun beating down on us. Wind. Not a hint of it. Outside or in. Breathe, I can't BREATHE!

The nice(er) guy I thought I knew displayed zero compassion for fresh meat and a particular zeal for following barked sideline orders. He'd hit me so hard it knocked the wind out of me and sent me crumpled back so far behind the line I could've been lined up to punt. My eyes bulged. My mind reeled. My body malfunctioned.

Whistles blew. Laugher and cheers and jeers rang out.

"GODDAMN!" and "Did you SEE that?!" and "HOLY SHIT is he still alive?!"

Writhing and gasping fruitlessly for air. Brain and lungs and body immolation. What fresh hell is this?! Nothing's working!

Lifted into the air by my facemask. Familiar face, unfriendly, bellowing. Dad? No, but similarly loud and authoritative.

"BREATHE! NICK! BREATHE!"

Ah! Coach. I don't understand why he's mad - I'm the one suffocating?! Shaking me like a bag of potatoes. A sharp jab to the chest. Agony. Rage. REVENGE!

A gutteral "yeeeeeeaaaarrrrggghhh!!!!" unlike any sound I'd ever made as angry lungs reinflated and an immediate lunge towards my... formerly underestimated adversary. Meaty middle school mathematician bearpaw holding me back.

"DAMNIT, STOP! WAIT, NICK! CALM DOWN! WAIT FOR THE WHISTLE!"

I was going to murder this guy. I didn't care that he stood a foot taller than me. I didn't care that he just flattened me like a pancake. I didn't care, didn't hear, didn't see anything but revenge.

Tossed back into the O-Line and encouraged to use it.

"GET HIM, JUMBO! GET... HIIIIIIM!!!!"

Quarterback called for the ball, this time I'm ready. Come and get some you smiling, slimy piece of...

Oh look... the sunset hasn't chased away all the blue from the sky. Gosh it's hot, but that sudden breeze is... nice. Wait. What was I doing? Why is everything all silent and woozy?

Thud. My body impacting the ground brought me back to reality. More sliding. More pain. More confusion. And then... even more rage.

The PREPUBESCENT BALLS on this guy! How DARE he knock me down again! This is supposed to be a friendly scrimmage! Same team, same team! I roared up off the ground and the rampage spectacle continued. Teammates and coaches holding me back. That sunnuva's gonna wish he'd never put on his pads! He's gonna be singing soprano the rest of his agonizingly short life! HOW ABOUT A LITTLE FIRE, SCARECROW?! LET ME AT HIM!!!

I was angrier than I had ever been in my life. I was completely out of control and enraged beyond any rational return. This was brutal. This was wrong. This was war.

Never again. I would not be put down ever again. He would not do it a third time. Who did this overgrown beanpole think he was, anyway? Nobody treats an Irish American like this and lives to tell about it. Certainly, no overgrown birch sapling from the wrong side of the tracks, certainly no poser who ran with the rough crowd but posed no... threat... SOMEBODY has to put him in his place... someone HAS TO DRAW THE LINE!

Aaaaaand touchdown. Not pigskin and celebratory whooping. No six points or high fives or butt slaps. Just more hollering. And laughing. And torment.

I'd been blasted back off the offensive line like a portly cannonball out of Gettysburg's darkest nightmare for the sake of protecting a sixteen-ounce piece of inedible pork three excruciating times in a row, and it all took less than three minutes.

I felt like I'd been run over by the tackle sled. And Coach's beautiful burnt orange 1977 Pontiac Grand Am. And a freight train. There wasn't a bone in my body that didn't hurt. I was bleeding. I was pounded into the ground by my ignorance and then my arrogance.

And then I was benched.

The molten tears of rage that tore down my sweaty cheeks were hotter than the boiled egg bleachers just a few feet behind me. For all of my fury, for all of my effort... I was defeated. I wasn't the invincible hulking brute my temper made me feel like. I wasn't the Incredible Hulk. I wasn't stronger. I wasn't the immovable mass met by the unstoppable force. I wasn't anything but defeated.

Or so I thought.

It turns out the Coach's reasoning for the scrimmage was a test, but not the same one my cooked and shook'd, rattled and clattered seventh grade brain assumed it to be.

As we were all "hustling" back to the locker room after practice, some of us limping and grimacing and cursing all the way, a young hand clapped down on my shoulder pad and a toothy grin flashed at me as it would for almost every sighting when our paths crossed in the hallways throughout our remaining middle and high school years.

"Welcome to the O-line!" Chris congratulated me. Confused and still mad at my mortal enemy, my expression must've been as confused and broken as the rest of my body was. "Coaches kinda like players who don't give up, you know?" He winked at me and trotted ahead to catch up with the raucous and wildly victorious eighth graders.

I'd made the team.

I let more tears fall.

Sometimes our perceived worst enemies turn out to be on our team after all. Sometimes the trials we suffer might be different from the tests we're truly taking.

THE POWER OF A SMILE

I was never the most popular kid in school.

As a matter of fact, I was most often the most overlooked.

I was good enough in band class to play the hardest instrument. But my father made it clear that my silly shiny horn wouldn't be paying any bills anytime soon, so I should enjoy the hobby while it lasted – and forget about honking it at home for any semblance of practice.

Okay, so not the best at math or P.E. either, decent enough at English, excellent at lunch and recess. Excellent at sucking up to adults, especially the ones in charge.

Being in rollie-pollie mode since the first grade made me target numero uno for the class bullies. Until I figured out that if I made fun of myself before anyone else could, I was somewhat immune from their hatred.

After all, who could hate a clown more than the one staring right through him in the mirror?

I managed to kiss enough supervisory ass at my middle school to get away with practically anything I wanted to, which was usually nothing more criminal than walking the halls whenever I wanted, a free milkshake or second helping from the lunch ladies, an extended grace period on an overdue library book, extra bathroom breaks, or an extra few minutes in the computer lab.

As my eighth-grade year was winding down, I managed to get nominated for a citizenship award of some sort. Apparently being the rotund class clown was a form of popularity I hadn't counted on. So, the adults in the school decided to award me for being the proverbial nice guy. The smiler. All friends, no enemies.

The celebrated fool.

At a ceremony in the gymnasium towards the end of the school day near the end of the school year, the three class-years of students and parents and teachers looked on as awardees were called up to receive their various honors and certificates of awesomeness. Front and center marched all manner of math geniuses, shop class prodigies, athletes and authors and scholars, oh my!

Looking at these lauded peers I began to feel... special? Like them? In good company? Similar? Dare I say... elite? Nay, cool?

One tragedy of self-loathing is that it tends to catapult one into a xenophobic sense of unique, mandated suffering - "I suffer because I deserve it, God wants it, or destiny wills it - whatever the source it is sacrosanct and my cross to bear, my burden alone."

Maybe my humor was... making a difference? Maybe my self-deprecation was a part of the greater good and made people feel better about themselves? Maybe Jesus made me this way so I could make the rest of His children feel better about themselves and life in general?

From my perch at the top of the bleachers I looked down on the immense flock of sheeple. My audience. My fans. I took a deep breath as my name was called. How could this be? How could someone earning an award in front of peers and parents and teachers be the same vilified worthless hunk of human meat-waste the mirror's reflection constantly loathed?

I had fooled them all. I had conquered their sneers and jeers and earned a place at the front table and my moment of triumph would be gleaming for years to come and a mural of my antics would be painted on the gymnasium wall and… and… is that another foot…

I had always chosen the top bleacher as a perfect perch so no one could sneak up behind me. So no one could look at me without me seeing them look at me first. It was safe. I was safe. I was… doomed.

One of the aforementioned class bullies graced me with what, up until that moment in my life, was the greatest perspective adjustment I had ever experienced. In an act of wanton, blatant, wholly intentional attempt to harm, maim, or otherwise dismember, cruelly tripped me as I took my first step down from the top bleacher. His timing was perfect.

My life would never be the same.

The first impact shook me so hard I think I stopped breathing. I heard a tremendous crash reverberating off the gymnasium walls that sounded like piles of wood being dropped from a tremendous height. It was the first of many such explosions.

The second impact a few bleachers down was equally jarring, and… oops. Yeah. Breathing again. The return of oxygen to my system began to invigorate pain receptors in my body and they began howling reports of impact tremors and damage in lightning-fast waves of excruciating vigor.

The third impact made time itself slow to an agonizing crawl. I was fairly certain this was a real-world exercise in mass, velocity, and gravity – but then again, my science grades weren't the best, either. Health class had taught me that human biology was not necessarily designed for... Herculean kangaroo bleacher bouncing sports... and... and... wait...

Impact number four, and a terrible realization wracked my brain harder than the screaming pain was – this particular maneuver was taking place with zero attitude, yaw, or heading control whatsoever (thank you flight simulation computer games), and suddenly my path was not so clear...

The blonde-haired girl had a name that meant the world to me. Her smile was like birds singing. Her laugh was generous. Her spirit was... descended from truly good heavenly characters the world had never nor may ever see again. Her grandmother had given me handfuls of balloons and suckers and stickers and hug after hug after hug at the local grocery store since I was old enough to walk, and we had gone to school together since kindergarten and I'd sat behind her in so many classes and she was the best artist I had ever... seen... and she played flute in band class... and... oh God...NO!

Harmony was the innocent iceberg just floating along making the surrounding Atlantic jealous of her incredible, shimmering beauty and... and... Nick O'TITANIC OF BOUNCY BOUNCE DOOM DEATH KILLER was hurtling towards her at nearly literal breakneck speed and...

The horror sank in as, ironically, Irish-descendant human-grade flesh-plate wasn't squishy enough to wobble thisly or thusly... ("ICEBERG DEAD AHEAD!") to brush past her glorious blonde curls and strike the nameless, faceless victim next to her – no. That would've been miraculous and merciful. Instead, as it did in April of

1912, the audacity of human arrogance was afforded a perspective adjustment in the form of an incredible, terrible impact.

The slow motion of my human blubber boulder thundering into Harmony's sweet, innocent frame only exacerbated the pain – but this was a pain of unmitigated terror that is a powerlessness to save innocent bystanders from the stupidity of an uncontrolled descent into Hell by this pitiful creature once stupid enough to believe he was special enough to be celebrated and would do anything to keep from hurting anyone at any time for any... reason... and... and...

More impacts. A ricochet off of a harmonious, innocent shoulder, and back onto the mostly clear path of wooden butcher block human cube-steak face, arm, stomach, leg, back, neck... everything became hazy. I can't hear anything now... but... when will it end?! BOOM!

Boom.

Boom.

Close your eyes. It'll all be over soon.

Boom.

Boom.

... boom.

... ...

boom?

Mesopotamian ziggurat miracle mile skyscraper of bleachered death – have mercy on this pitiful clown!

Into the void.

67

Hello darkness, my old friend.

A twinge.

Wait… what… is that… sound?

A wave?

I can't see anything.

I can't… smell… anything.

I taste something… warm. Something in my mouth? Warm. Metallic. Yep. Blood. That's blood.

What is that… SOUND? I feel… surrounded by… am I… under water?

I was not on a beach. But something is… crashing… towards me?

As if breaching like a Humpback Whale, the sensation of sound came crashing down on me like a drippy landing mammal of unfathomable tonnage.

It was laughter.

Riotous, cacophonic, deafening laughter as if Heaven's own choir of angels was howling in delight at this crumpled waste of human excrement lying in a discarded heap on the gymnasium floor.

It was a sound like nothing I had ever heard. The power. The magnitude. The volume.

The laughter was reverberating off of the gymnasium walls. It was shaking. The. Rafters.

It was unrelenting. It was unwavering. It was… unforgiving.

It was child and adult alike. It was friend and foe; it was teacher and counselor and administrator and janitor and bus driver and parent and grandparent and… and… it was inescapable.

I opened my eyes in the most unimaginable pain I had ever experienced up to that point in my life. It took all of my strength to open my eyes after lying there for a moment absolutely motionless and bathed in wave after wave of sonic shame. I would not be able to dig myself a hole in that floor. I would not be able to joke my way out of this. I would not be able to escape like it never happened. I had no choice.

The first person I saw was Mrs. Merrill, the home economics teacher, standing just a few feet away. She was not laughing. After picking her jaw up off the floor mouthed the words "ARE YOU OKAY?!" in the most horrified facial expression I had ever seen any human being pull off.

I blinked a few times and took a deep breath. The physical pain of battered eighth grade tub-o-lard body damage was nothing compared to the Krakatoan level public humiliation I'd just managed to demonstrate.

How in the hell would I recover from this? There had only been a few examples of this level of public spectacle ever in recorded human history, and I was fairly certain public pillory displays had been outlawed several centuries ago. At least I don't remember seeing any stockades or guillotines on the school playground during recess or P.E. or football practice. What could I do?

I could've laid there. I could've let the adults come to their senses and rush to my aid in a responsible, caring, and proper response. I could've let on that my body, though relatively round and apparently

69

disgustingly enormous, was indeed still quite capable of being damaged after a fall down every single bleacher from the tallest possible height.

I could've let forth a roar of rage and hatred and anger that would've shaken every last soul in that building to its very core. I could've… I could've…

I nodded "yes" at Mrs. Merrill. I took another deep breath.

And then I stood up.

I turned around and faced my heartless, hooting, hollering audience.

I looked immediately at Harmony to make sure she was okay. To this day I have never seen a more concerned, merciful, forgiving expression pointed back in my direction. Nor do I know if my spectacular fall truly hurt her. She denied it every time I ever asked her about it again for years following the event.

Knowing she was okay; I then turned my attention to the throngs of cackling onlookers. Knee slapping and high fives and tears of joy.

I smiled.

Out of every possible, every situationally-acceptable reaction option, I chose to smile.

It wasn't fair. It wasn't nice. Go ahead. Laugh at my pain. That's why I was put here for you all.

I smiled.

I shrugged.

I limped up and collected my award certificate.

I nodded in thanks at the teachers and administrators leading the presentation.

I limped back to the bleachers.

I chose a seat on the first level this time.

I made it out of the gymnasium and home alive in one piece later that same day.

And to this day?

I have never forgotten the power of a smile.

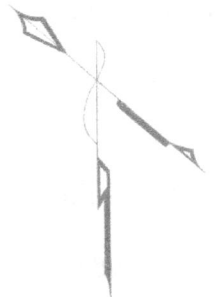

CHEX MARKS THE WAISTLINE SPOT

Tradition.

Every year about this time there is a push in America to remember the traditions of yore, to honor the past in the present, and celebrate that which is most cherished in typical American households: holidays, family, and food.

Enter... the Chex Mix.

My mother makes her weight in homemade Chex Mix every year. Why? Because she prefers rotund children. Because she is a glutton for serving delicious punishment. Because she is a crack dealer.

I simply cannot get enough of this stuff. Before it was readily available on grocery store shelves year-round, Mom's homemade Chex Mix was the bellringer of the coming of Christmas, good times, and all-around improved happiness. Everyone who samples some likes it. Everyone who tries some can't have JUST some - inevitably their hand(s) end up back into the Mix and shoveling loads of it into their mouth like a front loader dumping salt into a dump truck for Hoosier winter county road clearing.

She takes it with her everywhere. Family get-togethers of course, but there is no limit to the woman's Chex Mix pestilence-spreading ambition. Grocery stores, card games, CHURCH... she's always got a little bag of it with her wherever she goes. It's like her seasonal good luck charm.

It's good luck for her and BAD NEWS for anyone who succumbs to the temptation of "oh, okay, maybe just a bite." Then you're hers! You've forgotten your woes, forgotten the seasonal nerve strain, forgotten everything - even how to chew and talk simultaneously. I've seen its effect on countless people throughout the years... the momentary assumption that you've had Chex Mix before, what's the big deal... a tentative nibble and a few more, suddenly your eyes widen and heaven's light shines down on you and then you're in the middle of the grocery store having a religious experience with several fellow strangers/victims surrounding you and the Chex Mix pusher like it's a sponsored industry taste test and eventually you all look like a flock of squirrels who've finally found their winter's stash in March. And in the center is my mother, beaming. Grinning from ear to ear and reveling in delight that her Chex Mix Army has just added another battalion for her global domination efforts.

She takes her culinary vengeance out on spinners and pickers the most. I am a spinner, hunting for anything but the Melba toast crumbles and Brazil nuts. My pinnacle prey are the cashews and sticky orbs of seasoning usually sticking to the Wheat Chex.... Oooooooo the goosebumps that cover my trembling arms just imagining that drop of savory, salty goodness, and the tumble of cashew nut glory upon my tongue! If I had a dollar for every time she scolded me for my pesky Chex Mix bits picking-and-choosing habits, I'd have enough capital to sponsor her year-round culinary industrialization of this dichotomy of waistline destruction/taste bud intoxication.

Thankfully there is a limit to the amount she makes. I know because

73

eventually the Chex cereal boxes start disappearing around her house and my waistline breathes a momentary sigh of relief. The theme park rollercoaster of my Type 2 diabetes obliteration finds a momentary merciful plateau. Suddenly I can focus again, I can pay attention when I'm driving, I can be productive at work...

But wait a minute! Just when you think you've had enough, she's upped the ante! She's made an alteration to the witch's brew of spices and strength of them to make Chex Mix version 2.0. Then 3.0. And soon you might as well take a handful of varying Chex cereals, a handful of mixed nuts, and the Lea & Perrins Worcestershire sauce and shovel them into your mouth all at once because by this point it's like you haven't had your fix in years. Even though you've gained twenty pounds on the stuff since Thanksgiving and it's become its own food group.

I love my mother. Dearly. She is the one person on this planet who is most responsible for the man and a half I am today. I admire her spirit, her heart, her effect on people, and her kitchen magic. But what she unleashes on this planet every year around this time is a tidal wave of savory addictive goodness that invades your very consciousness, challenges the heavens and hells for possession of your very soul... and if you dare attempt break yourself away from the pull of her incredible concoction before its saddled you with a spare tire of added girth around your waist, you will find yourself hungry for something you can't quite identify... something between meals that is good enough to maybe even be a meal... something that takes you back to the bygone era of simpler times and home and hearth and family and... and...

What was I saying?

*munch, munch, munch

PARENTAL PRESENTS OF MIND

When I was in 6th or 7th grade, I got a Starter jacket for Christmas.

Many people may not remember the status symbol of Starter jackets back in those bygone days, but if you had one? WOW! You were the EPITOME of cool! I was fairly obsessed with an NFL quarterback named Randall Cunningham of the Philadelphia Eagles in the late 1980's and early 1990's, and back then the guy was on fire. He practically invented NFL QB swagger. Not only that, he had the arm AND LEGS to prove it! The guy was good in an era of mostly forgettable NFL teams and he's the reason I watch the Eagles with a somewhat interested eye even today.

So, my parents lovingly ensured my Christmas morning was one for the ages - and I adored that jacket more than any other possession I had ever owned. I walked around school with it on like I owned the joint. I winked at pretty girls, I hissed at the school bullies. That coat was my armor. My everything. As long as I was wearing it nothing could stop me. I was invincible. The coal-black mass, highlighted by the shimmering green "EAGLES" script on the back, the single Bald Eagle soaring on the left front breastplate toting a football... to this day I remember the instant badassery that was myself donned in that jacket. I was Iron Man without the billions. I was Superman without the muscles. I was... I was...

A fool.

Vulnerable to the magic of the coat and Cunningham's example, I began to rebel against my father at home in the form of dishonesty. I would lie about everything.

"What did you get on your social studies homework?" - Dad "An A." - Me

"Let me see it."

"The teacher kept it."

"Why?"

"It was so good he wanted to use it as an example for the other students."

"I'm hungry." - Me

"Did you have an after school snack?" - Dad

"No."

"But all of the hotdogs are gone."

"I had to feed the cats."

"Why would you feed hotdogs to cats?"

"Because we were out of cat food." "Why are we out of cat food?"

"I dunno, ask Mom."

"I'm still hungry." - Me

"No, you're not. You're bored." - Dad

"I had smaller portions than everyone else!"

"No, you just inhaled it like a vacuum cleaner and didn't slow down and chew your food."

"How would you know what a vacuum cleaner does? I've never seen you touch ours."

"What?"

"Nothing."

Eventually my father caught me in one of my most inane fallacies and he had had enough. He didn't slave away at the gear factory blast furnaces, sweating his life away day after day after day, just to have his plump brat son lie to him about everything from food to grades to chore reports. And he was right. How do I know he was right? Because I've been a parent before. Even as a stepparent, nothing infuriated me more than being lied to, no matter how trivial the subject was. It was insulting, it was wasting time, and it was wrong. I was wrong.

So, to teach me a lesson, that Spring, my father dragged the metal trash can out from the garage and built a fire in it. He called me outside and confronted me about the lie (to this day I don't remember the exact straw that broke the camel's back). Of course, I compounded the crime by lying about the lie. It was all the evidence he needed. He told me to collect my beloved Starter jacket and wrap it in a paper grocery bag and come outside. I did so. He told me to hand it over. I did so. He tossed the bag into the trash can. An inferno consumed the paper bag. And my very being.

I had never felt despair like that before ever in my life. Sure, I had lamented when grandparents fell ill, when church members passed away, and when I injured myself; but this was a violation. This was unholy terror. He had to restrain me from jumping into the trash can to save my armor, my life, my everything. The raging tears that burned my face were only bested in power by the hideous wailing bullhorning from my enraged beak. I was despondent, I was enraged, and I was fooled.

As I stood there blubbering over a ninety-dollar coat in a time when gasoline was still so cheap a twenty-dollar bill would be more than enough to fill the family's car gas tank, we were so poor it was Hamburger Helper for dinner three or four nights a week. My despair and anguish was only mirrored in my father's own tears. What a terrible position to be in as a parent—to love someone so much that you have to hurt them to keep them from hurting themselves. Dad tossed another paper bag at me. Because I was a far cry from the quarterback idol I had been looking up to for so long, I dropped it. My tears had all but totally washed out the oncoming impact from my vision. I waited for more punishment, more impacts, more anything. I was wasted. I was worthless. I was nothing without that Starter jacket, but the damage was done. The lesson was learned.

The undamaged, unburned Starter jacket was laying at my feet.

Dad had tossed a decoy paper bag full of old newspapers into the conflagration instead of my beloved Starter jacket and social armor.

"I love you too much to let you go on lying your way through life," Dad said. "When you lie to me, you hurt me. When you lie to me, you're saying: 'I don't love you enough to tell you the truth.' Stop lying to everyone, son. You're better than this, and now you know what it feels like to be lied to."

I will never forget that day. And I will never forget the lesson. Love isn't always about hugs and kisses and Sunday school and Christmas presents. Sometimes it means terrible consequences for parents and children alike. But I still believe it's worth it.

Hug someone you love today. You never know when your love will mean a pain you can hardly bear but will have to endure. Or when a hug will be the most cherished, most valuable, but most unavailable expression of love you will never again share in this world.

I love you, Dad.

Thanks for loving me too much to let me lie.

R/T: TARGET ACQUIRED

I had been staring at her for the past three weeks. Online only, my girlfriend had no idea. I felt guilty - it was like my dirty little secret. And then every time I climbed into my 2012 Dodge Challenger SXT I felt guilty again, telling myself it was good enough, it was fast enough, why was I even thinking of a different car? Friends and coworkers were on both sides of the fence: "you only live once," and "so it's red, what's wrong with the white one," "DUDE! HEMI!" and "four years to pay off versus seven? Are you crazy?!" I was waffling back and forth like Sunday morning breakfast.

"Life's too short to drive boring cars..." playing over and over in my head, quickly followed by "not that the SXT is boring..."

So, I eventually confessed my vehicular indiscretion to my girlfriend. I didn't need her approval, but I value her opinion and honesty, and much to my surprise she didn't squash it immediately with an unholy feminine logic monster. I knew then something had to be happening deep in the universe, conspiring to make something big happen...

Off to the dealership we go. We both took the day off, drove an hour to see it, talking on the way about why it had been sitting on the lot for three months, was a local one-owner trade, and the differences between an SXT and an R/T. We talked finances, of course, and how this decision could and would affect us for years to come. I told her the story of how I found the SXT, bought it, took it to the local dealership to get the plastic rocker panels replaced two weeks later and saw an Anniversary R/T in the showroom and nearly burst into tears because I could've had it instead. And then... and then...

We pulled into the dealership and saw her. The sunlight had all but disappeared into overcast, but that red... that High Octane Red Pearl Coat... that black and maroon beauty short-circuited our brain buckets into useless masses of meat. My girlfriend just kept asking me "Is that it? Are you sure that's the one? It can't be. Are you serious? There's no way we can afford that car. They're gonna want three thousand dollars down for that thing!" The salesman ran the numbers while we took it for a test drive.

I popped the trunk on the initial walkaround and saw a cardboard box with a factory airbox in it. I thought, "That's odd, why would they disconnect that?" I looked at the tailpipes, I thought, "Those aren't stock..." I shrugged off the aft anomalies and climbed into the driver's seat next to my girlfriend who was strangely silent. She had wide eyes and was touching everything from the oh shit handle, to the floor mats, twisting and turning in every direction in the passenger seat, opening the sunroof shade, glovebox, console, backseat armrest storage compartment, and then I started it...

The specs? One local owner 2014 Dodge Challenger R/T plus 100th Anniversary Edition, six thousand one hundred on the clock, 5.7-liter HEMI, five-speed auto-stick, Super Track Pak, 3.06 rear end, Corsa Billet Catback Exhaust, Mopar Cold Air Intake, ~ four hundred HP...

The growl. That moment. The look on my girlfriend's face. My pounding chest. I thought I was ready. I thought I was prepared. I thought I could handle it. I knew nothing. This was pure emotion. This was raw power. This was carnal, this was savage, this was before we left the dealer's lot!

We pulled out onto the highway. I babied the throttle up to fifty five miles per hour. Right turn onto another highway. Exhaust notes intoxicating on downshifts. Every crack in the road is discernible in the driver's seat. This couldn't be the same car that the SXT was. It wasn't even close! This was heart pounding, pissed off cougar in the backseat, caged monster under the hood, fevered joyride "please God don't let me scratch this thing before the ink's dry" Millennium Falcon jump-to-lightspeed was that just seventy-five miles per hour on the gauge; everything's a blur!

Stoplight. Red. Thank God. Deep breath. Green light, half throttle, girlfriend yelps as back tires chirp, she's sold. Back to the dealership. Easy on the entry, try not to smile so big, face hurts from epic grin, heart still pounding.

Something that exciting had to be sinful. Nothing in my twenty years of driving had prepared me for that onslaught. That obliteration of logic. That... raw power, that sound, that... that complete conversion to the dark side.

Now to get her home.

Every sin has its price. I thought I was prepared to pay. I thought I'd considered every possible financial angle. I thought wrong. As usual my girlfriend had maintained a measure of intelligence when I had been reduced to a four-year-old OOOOHHH SHINY MINE MINE MINE!

Dealership wanted six times the down payment I was prepared to give. Dealership wanted to give me only two thirds of what I needed for my trade. Chrysler Financial wanted an interest rate almost three times my maximum number.

We drove home in the SXT. Sunset in the sky, midnight in the car. Near silence until the inevitable blow-up. One thousand five hundred silly dollars' difference after hours of negotiation separated us from the car of my dreams...the car of OUR dreams. What happened? What the hell just happened? This can't be! This has to be a nightmare...

A sleepless night. I didn't need the R/T, I had a solid, dependable, attractive, fast enough daily driver... but what if? Just what if? Damn that dealer! Didn't I deserve the R/T? Didn't WE deserve the R/T?

Resolve. It's not their car... it is MY DESTINY!

Nine AM I'm back at the dealership. At noon I'm driving home in the R/T. Mine. Monthly payment is twenty dollars more than SXT was. Down payment was twice what I originally offered. Interest rate two points above SXT rate. Paid thousands under Kelley Blue Book value.

Tearing up country roads in sparkly maroon R/T THUNDER has been more joy than I can remember in any vehicle since my teenage years.

And as for my girlfriend? She saw it in the sunshine for the first time yesterday. She had tears in her eyes.

Once in a lifetime purchase. Made mostly on my terms.

Game officially changed.

NASHVILLE

The Music City.

Forget whatever you've heard about this town. Unless you've been here, you might not understand what I'm about to say, but I'll say it anyway.

This town never knew a stranger.

Since my arrival on Thursday, I have never been afraid. I have never been harassed. I have never felt threatened. I have never felt alone.

On the contrary, this town is chock full of people ready to help, serve, protect, shuttle, feed, and entertain each and every last guest they meet.

Have you ever been in a place since your childhood that felt so familiar and safe you could swear you've been there before, knowing you've never been? Like you know all the shortcuts and the best restaurants and parties and people to see that wasn't your hometown?

This is Nashville.

Live music EVERYWHERE!

I saw a gorgeous, long-haired blonde violinist nailing "The Devil Went Down to Georgia," doing a Texas two-step slash Irish jig maneuver on top of a makeshift wooden platform wearing the tightest blue jeans and biggest smile I've ever seen. On the sidewalk. For quarters and nickels and dimes. Not at The Opry. Not on a stage. On the sidewalk. And she was loving every minute of it.

I saw a group of African immigrants punishing five-gallon buckets with drumsticks, the likes of which would put the Stomp Broadway show to utter shame and ruin.

I saw so many live bands singing their hearts out like they were saving the world with their song. Loud. Passionate. Raw. Energy!

I saw so many smiles and hugs and high fives and embraces. It erased the depression of my hometown football warriors' forty-nine-point slaughter at the Music City Bowl by the "other Alabama team."

I saw a Nashville Predators jersey-clad "real man" get put down by a smaller, younger bouncer. The same bouncer picked the man up and helped him back to the curb not thirty seconds later and they were hugging it out. All within my first hour in this town.

I saw sports rival fans treating each other with courtesy, respect, and yes... pity. I did not see a single fight off the field in the stadium, on the streets, or in any bar.

The alcohol flows like a river through this town. It's like a religion here - not to numb the pain of existence and life, but instead to lubricate any hesitation of happiness.

And anyone downtown is ready to put you into a cab or an Uber at any moment to make sure you get home safe.

Speaking of which, Uber drivers here are friendly, abundant, and generous with their smiles, suggestions, and locale expertise.

I saw a woman on stage last night in a bar that was the definition of "in her element." She had a good voice, but no superstar. She had flowing, long blonde hair and a stunning smile. She had presence. Command. Grace. Charm. She could've turned the roaring crowd into a mob at any moment, but instead, enthralled and entertained them. Total control of the place. For pennies and dollar bills in a bucket. She was absolutely enchanting.

I will never forget Nashville.

Not because I made it here with a good friend and my Boilers didn't bother to show up. Not because the Titans' stadium has an amazing pedestrian bridge to arrive on, where I greeted and shook hands with my hometown mayor as he walked into the game with the rest of the crowd. Not because I haven't even scratched the surface of the throng of places left to visit, an entire town left to explore. Not because of music or food or fun.

I will never forget Nashville because, for the first time since I can remember, this town is full of humans being.

Put Nashville, Tennessee on your destination list, friends! I promise this southern belle will grab your heart and never let go!

Part 3: Surviving

For all of the flowery words used in the last two section summaries, the largest section of this book is surely the most fittingly titled.

I may talk a good game when it comes to how different artists may be, and how all it takes is a bit of imagination to transform the mundane daily march into a gleaming glimpse of flawed, delicious humanity. But there are times in life where all of those grandiose words have to take a backseat to every human's ultimate pursuit – Survival.

Admittedly most of the circumstances and events in this last section of the book are follies of my own making. As I have often been chided, sometimes I am "too smart for my own good, and too dumb to get out of my own way." My choice in vehicles and their occupants are sometimes to blame. Other times I am as much at the mercy of Mother Nature as anyone else.

Self-inflicted or otherwise, here is a collection of stories aimed at the survival of the un-fittest.

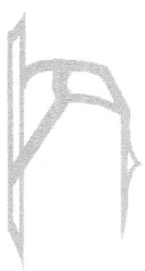

B-DUBS DEBACLE

I got a message from a high school friend on Facebook asking me if I wanted to grab some wings at B-Dubs and catch up. After her shaky instructions on getting to "her" house, she stumbles - not walks, or skips, or runs, but *stumbles* to my car. As soon as she gets in, she proceeds to light a cigarette. The smell of alcohol on her breath is overpowering and I'm trying to be optimistic as I'm passionately encouraging her to put her cigarette out the window as I don't allow cigarettes to be smoked in my thirty-thousand-dollar dream car. We make it to B-Dubs, but not before she reminds me of a marching band incident in high school where I once backed into her during a show and collided with her instrument so hard it caused her to have a major nosebleed.

At the restaurant, she makes a complete ass of herself. She slaps me on the back of the head when I tell her I'm a Colts fan (she's Bears), I'm a Cubs fan (no smack there), and I lie and tell her the Blackhawks are my NHL pick (no favorite NHL team). She argues with the bartender about what to put in her mixed shots, of which she has two. One is Goldschlager and Jager, the other is Goldschlager and Grand Mariner as she sips on a Coors Light draft beer.

By this point it's been an hour into the adventure, and to bail myself out, I tell her I got paged by my employer and I need to come in to fix a label printer. I don't feel guilty about this in the slightest since she was truly making a scene at the bar, and the bartender was an idiot who should've cut her off. Even with just the two shots and one third of a beer, she is severely inebriated and argues with me that I should bring her with me to my employer while I fix the broken printer.

After an order of boneless buffalo wings to-go that she proceeds to open and devour mercilessly and an hour of arguing about how I should either take her to my house (oh... *HELL* no), or leave her there at the restaurant and come pick her back up after I'm finished at work, she offers to take a cab, even though she's so broke she can't afford the tip on the forty-dollar "meal" we've just "shared" (my portion being a single unsweetened iced tea). I help her to the ladies' room, I do NOT follow her in, she spends five minutes doing God knows what in there, and when she comes out, she acts almost sober.

...that is until we get to the restaurant entryway where she collapses like a big top circus tent deflating without warning. Just...*BOOM*! She falls and falls hard.

She begins writhing and convulsing uncontrollably on the floor, sputtering obscenities and some unholy language the gods forgot four hundred years before the Romans adopted Christianity as their official religion. I scream at the restaurant CHILDREN who are working that night to stop staring at the gross spectacle and dial 911 on their handy telephone. I'm trying to keep her from bashing her head in on the wall, there are people coming in and out of the restaurant with the most horrified expressions on their faces, and the train wreck is only just beginning.

Two of the city's finest are on the scene within minutes. They are as helpless as I am watching my "friend" seize on the ground uncontrollably, still incoherent and eyes rolling back into her skull. We keep her on her side so she doesn't aspirate. She is fighting so hard against us the wall is buckling under her maneuvers.

Paramedics arrive just as she's sputtering "Grand Mal" something or other, and she's raging against the medics who refuse to put up with her bullshit. They are all saying "meth" and "controlled substance" and all kinds of diagnoses - nothing about Grand Mal seizures. They are telling her she's NOT having a Grand Mal seizure, and that if she doesn't stop fighting them all like some pissed off grizzly bear, they will sedate her and forcibly restrain her. They get her in the ambulance where she continues to shriek like a banshee.

The cops are nice but extremely suspicious of me. Understandably, my story of seeing her twice in the last twenty years (and the previous sighting at a church the day before) is a weak one, but they can tell by my own horrified expression that I am simply the idiot who bought her dinner.

At the hospital, she continues to rage against the machine until she is sedated several moments later - or, at least, I was told she was. At 11:30 PM when I finally get to see her she looks at me like I'm a two-headed monster and screams, "YOU'RE NOT REAL!" at me. She starts slamming and kicking the bed and ripping off her leads. With alarms wailing, in comes the goon squad to subdue her, and I go back out into the waiting room.

On a hunch, I ask the nurse out there if she had any emergency contact info on file. Lo and behold, she lives with her father, but they have zero contact info for him on file since the landline phone listed was probably disconnected years ago. He was a teacher at my high school. I even graduated with his son (her older brother), and now I have to drive my idiot ass back to HIS house and tell him about this glorious evening and the writhing, incensed, werewolf-esque, howling creature in the ER that is/was his little girl.

I arrive at their house, and not only does he come to the door, her two boys (aged nine and six) show up, too. I have to tell them their mother and daughter is in the ER with seizures. He asks me to go back to the hospital with them, so I do as he's an incredibly good man and I have always respected him. He asks me if she had been drinking. It's midnight, and we're still standing at his front door. I tell him what she had to drink. His eyes drop and his heartbreak is palpable: "I told her no alcohol."

He loads up the kids into the minivan in their PJ's. We arrive back at the ER, and I swear on everything I am, we can hear her screaming as the automatic doors pull open. She sounds like the Exorcist girl gone more mental. He asks me to watch the kids in the waiting area, and of course, I do.

By some miracle, they are two of the coolest kids I have ever met. I deduce it has everything to do with being raised by their grandfather and nothing to do with their mother. We keep it light-hearted: "Where do you go to school?" "What's your favorite subject?" "Yes, Mommy is a raging alcoholic who is mixing her MDD, MAD, and sleep disorder medicines with a potent yet mysterious alcohol cocktail and is fighting the people trying to save her life," you know, appropriate things past midnight on a school night in the ER with my high school "friend's" terrified children.

Her dad comes out and reassures the boys she's going to be okay, the doctors are helping her, and that Mommy's gonna take a nap now. He pulls me aside and asks me again what exactly happened. He says she has claimed someone slipped something into her drink at the bar. All the blood drains from my face and I tell him no one else was at the bar but her, the bartender, and me. I adamantly and truthfully tell him it certainly was not me or the bartender - some scared lookin' kid ironically named "Maverick" - our high school mascot - who couldn't even make her shots right let alone slip anything in her 2.3 drinks.

He nods and looks understanding. He asks me to stay with the boys for a while until she's calmed down. The kids and I go back to talking about how Cartoon Network has new cartoons on Thursday, how one of their favorite Star Wars' characters is Darth Vader while the other, of course, is that goodie two-shoes Luke Skywalker, and we get drinks of water in coffee cups out of the waiting room bathroom sink.

Dad finally comes back out after about forty-five minutes and announces she's finally asleep, and they're going home. The boys look sad because they didn't get to see their mom. I told them don't be afraid; she'll be okay. They actually *hug me*, and her dad takes my phone number and nearly hugs me himself. With tears in his eyes, he tells me how he's been praying something would break the cycle and that God would show her she has things worth living for. He thanks me for being a friend and not taking advantage of the situation (to which I nearly explode in tears myself) and apologizes for the nuclear fallout of an ordeal we've been through. He turns and shuffles off to take his amazing grandsons home.

It's 2:00 AM now. I check on her one more time, and she is indeed sleeping. I decide it's really in everyone's best interests that I do not disturb her, and I quietly make my exit. I go home, and my mother, worried sick, hugs me, cries, and tells me I'm a good man and a good friend. I still can't help but feel like I am somehow to blame for all this.

EPILOGUE: I wake up at 6:00 AM the next morning and replay the living nightmare in my mind over and over until I notice my cell phone blinking. It's my "date" from last night, texting me "thank you's" for abandoning her in her hour of greatest need at one hospital when she needed to be at another instead, and asking me why I cut and ran when things got real.

The moral of this story? Good guys not only finish last, they get blamed for everyone else's mistakes along the way, no good deed goes unpunished, and nothing good ever happens at B-Dubs past 9:00 PM on a weeknight.

CARMEX CARNAGE

Carmex.

For well over a decade, I've been loyal to Chapstick. Why? Cherry and strawberry trumps whatever the hell Carmex smells like. I HATE Carmex. The smell has been offensive to me for as long as I can remember. I have never tried it or Burt's Bees or anything other than Chapstick, medicated or regular.

Until today.

My lips have been perpetually chapped since, oh, about 1993. I used to blame it on playing brass instruments in various bands. I used to blame it on Indiana winters and humidity and sunburn and windburn and everything except the nervous habit I have of being a lip biter, skin picker, or other various and glorious human experiences.

Today at the cafe in my building, I was forced to relent. All they have available is Carmex. My bleeding lips screech in protest whenever my tongue or any other liquid passes over them like barbed fishhooks, tearing at the throbbing, swollen flesh.

Of course I may exaggerate a bit - but I can only assume my single relationship status has everything to do with my rotundity and other physical blessings including the daring-come-hither-do of shredded lip meat. And let's not get started on the mental Sahara slog that must be the burden of fencing with me on a daily basis.

But I digress.

Carmex acquired. Carmex applied. CARMEX HELL ON MY MOST TENDER FLESH!! AAAAAHHHHHH! SEARING SIZZLE ON THE HELL GRILL! MAKE IT STOP! AHHHHH! FOR THE LOVE OF ALL THINGS HOLY! HELLFIRE AND JALAPENO REVENGE!!

The menthol bath of healing salve instantly began the torture only my nose was once privy to. The smell of this devil goop was enough to keep me away for decades, why in the name of heaven did I do this to myself?! There is no God! Am I crying? My eyes ARE watering... someone save me from this torture!

My imagination begins making excuses. I lovingly kissed a habanero elder pepper. I cheese-grater'd my lips. There was an old-fashioned push mower that needed a smooch. I sipped a drink from Old Faithful. Is this what kissing Christina Hendricks feels like?

The throbbing was so intense I started feeling the pricklies in my collarbones and shoulders. I could hear my heartbeat. I thought for sure the pain would never end. Death by Carmex - a fitting end for a sad life!

But suddenly? Calm relief lapped upon my lips like a lazy noon tide coming in. The throbbing eased then vanished like it was never there. The pounding in my lips and ears subsided. The music went from Metallica's "KILL EM ALL!" to Enya's "Orinoco Flow." It was over mere minutes after the initial onslaught began.

Ahhhh! My lips feel so much better!

95

The line for kisses forms to the left and there IS a signup sheet, so please write legibly. And... sorry about the smell. Carmex SUCKS but wow... chapped lips are the worst!

I STRUGGLE

January 7, 2021

I struggle.

I struggle to quantify how I feel about this week in American history.

I struggle because I am a man full of passion.

I struggle because I am a man fighting an unknown (as of yet) illness.

I struggle because there is a fire in me that loves this country like nothing else.

Not because my hero grandfather fought for the US Army in World War II.

Not because my other grandfather was a United States Air Force and Strategic Air Command veteran.

Not because a man I currently love like a father also served in the United States Air Force.

Not because another man I call a dear friend also served in the US Army during Vietnam.

Or another beloved relative that served in the US Marines during Vietnam.

I struggle because I love a nation, a dream, and a way of life has become schizophrenic and tragically, dreadfully self-destructive.

I struggle because I am surrounded in physical location and family-friend affiliation mostly by members of a political party opposite of my own.

I struggle because some of their answers for seeking answers involve praying to, worshiping, paying, or bowing to a God I no longer believe in.

I struggle because I could not, in my wildest nightmares, ever imagine United States citizens invading and attempting to overthrow the government I have been loyal to for forty one years. As have countless members of both sides of my family for far longer.

I struggle because there are some people who decry identification of these traitors as being members of this group, or that group, when as far as I'm concerned only one label is sufficient for anyone who behaves in such treasonous ways: enemy of the state.

I struggle because people I have known and loved for months and years and decades are content to fall back on whataboutisms and claims of election corruption as excuses for mob mentality and sedition attempts.

I struggle because good people died attempting to protect the seat of my government.

I struggle because my feisty nature demands swift, severe retribution.

I struggle because the emotion in me wants the scaffolds returned to the Capitol. Hang every traitor from it in a national broadcast with a dire message written in blood above them: "the price of sedition" and lessons to be taught in every school that the Pledge of Allegiance is fine to memorize as long as you don't disagree with a presidential election result and then you can forget it and defecate and vandalize government buildings and threaten government officials until you get your way.

I struggle because I am thrown to the extreme from one cause to the next by a condition in modern American politics that demands an either-or definition, lesser of two evils, this OR that. Zero room for compromise, moderation, or peace.

I struggle because a friend's house was sprayed with bullets, another house down the road from them similarly attacked, and a local political party headquarters directly across the street from the county courthouse/county seat was also shot up.

I struggle because in my emotional reactions to all of this I am left with almost zero sense of personal responsibility.

But in my mind now, I do not struggle with the truth: we are all to blame.

There is no excuse for violence. In any human behavior, excluding self-defense.

I struggle to make sense of the chaos of the last ten years of my life, my liberty, and my pursuit of happiness - especially staring at these terrifying images on my TV.

But I must continue to struggle.

I will continue to struggle to force back the dragon in my heart that demands revenge for hurting the people and places I love.

I will continue to struggle to vow for peace and moderation and freedom for all Americans within the definitions of the law.

I will continue to struggle to listen to perspectives and priorities and preaching by fellow Americans I might not agree with on every idea, dream, faith, or method of pursuit(s).

I will continue to struggle to remember the reality that not everyone on the other side of every argument, perspective, faith, stance, idea, and-or background is my enemy.

I will continue to struggle with controlling my temper on the road with people who are too busy or too ignorant to follow those laws. Or at least too slow.

I will continue to struggle. Because my friends, my family, my life, and my country...

Are worth the struggle.

PIGEON FORGE

It was a romantic getaway.

Pigeon Forge, Tennessee was a bucket list destination for me, and my girlfriend at the time had been once before; "Heaven on Earth!" she called it.

Not the tourist trap of Gatlinburg. Not the hustle and bustle and hubbub of Nashville. Pigeon Forge was THE place to go.

A shortish drive from home, the land of Dolly Parton (a national treasure), restaurants and museums and mountain horseback rides and ATV adventures.

On top of all the majestic scenery, there was the added bonus of driving my new Dodge Challenger muscle car for the entire trip, designed for tearing up mountain roads and annoying the hell out of locals with a Mopar rumble tumbling down mountainsides as alternate thunder.

Another bonus was sketchy cell phone reception. No work emergencies. No family emergencies. Nearly total isolation, several hours' drive south from the day-to-day.

To call the scenery simply "majestic" earlier is a tragic understatement. For a flatlander born and raised in the glacially carved middle north of some of America's richest farmland, the elevation and even danger of some of those mountain passes was exhilarating. Almost no straight roads as far as the eye could see.

We were in love. We were child-free. We were on a real vacation. In our own rented cabin, the Smoky Mountains.

At one point during our exuberant exploring, we took a driving tour through Smoky Mountain National Park. With the sunroof open. In June. The sights and smells and sounds surrounding us were like nothing I'd ever experienced in my life. It was a challenge to keep my attention on the road. Old, abandoned houses and mills, rivers here, streams there, and beauty ever present in every direction I looked.

Another adventure took root on a road I will forever label "the goat path." The treacherous trip was white-knuckle; a harrowing, blind corners on a single gravel lane trek literally over a mountain, and eventually into a summit luxury log cabin construction site I can only imagine was millions of dollars in the making, and into the wide eyes and gaping maws of a bewildered construction crew.

"How in the HELL did you get THAT thing all the way up HERE?!" the foreman chided me.

"Prayer, sir. Lots and lots of prayer..." I replied.

We tiptoed as timidly and gently as possible back down the path Billies feared to tread after turning around to the cheers and jeers of the gobsmacked nailers. I have never before or since been more terrified behind the wheel of any vehicle I've ever driven.

Blood pressure checks accomplished, we retreated to the comfort of our rented cabin and took full advantage of the bubbly hot tub on the elevated porch overlooking some of the most breathtaking scenery I'd ever laid my eyes on.

Life was good. The adventures were thrilling. The chance to get away from it all was invaluable.

A curiosity I'd noticed upon our arrival was about to be solved, not that either of us was paying much attention. We were young and in love and enjoying the bubbles. I'll skip waxing poetic about this part for the faint of heart and/or stomach…

When we first pulled up to the cabin, I'd noticed some chains on the trash containers outside. I didn't think much of them; raccoon-proofing, I'd assumed. We found a key with instructions inside the cabin, directing us to put all trash into those containers at the conclusion of our stay, and to make sure - beyond all other tasks - to re-secure and relock the chains "WITHOUT FAIL."

Okay, the cabin owners liked to keep things tidy, I naively quipped. Pest control? Check.

The sounds and magic of an early summer Smoky Mountain dusk / romantic rendezvous surrounding us, this young Indiana couple were Jerry Lee Lewis mode in a hot tub of love and all was well with the world.

SNAP!

A somewhat muffled woodland rimshot rang out from the mountainside below us.

SHIFT shift wobble wobble... GRrrrrUNT! came the next blood-curdling mystery from directly below our elevated love nest.

At first I was sure I was hearing things. My girlfriend was many things, but these noises were beyond even her talents.

*Grnt grunt hmph... huff… HUFF! SNIFFFFFF... SNIFFFFFF....
yawnnnnnnnn!"

Okay now, I'm no lothario but a yawn is a bit mu...

"GRRRRRUNTTTTTT!"

We peeked out over the side of the hot tub, both almost frozen solid
with fear, even while surrounded by the burbling soup of a kissy
cauldron and probably even some poo at this point.

NOT a raccoon.

NOT a deer.

NOT a fox.

A very large... black bear.

Rumbling and bumbling directly beneath us.

I could just make out his ears and snout between the slats of the
wooden porch.

Not two feet below us.

DEFINITELY some poo at this point.

"HOW are we going to get back inside?!" my now very-much-hot-
and-bothered-for-very-different-reasons companion whispered
frightfully.

I was just as terrified as she was.

I'd seen enough nature documentaries in my life from the comfort of several Indiana homes (where bears were never to be found) to know that, aside from playing dead, the best way to avoid being mauled by a bear was to already BE dead, so my panic-stricken male brain deduced the only logical conclusion to be found at the moment: if we weren't bear kibble already, it was only a matter of moments before Fozzy ambled up the slope and onto the porch for his rosy pink hu-nugget supper.

I'm a big man. I tip the scales way north of two hundred pounds, and truth be told - Thanksgiving was generous this year, so let's just say I'm north of two hundred fifty pounds and leave it at that. My girlfriend at the time was curvy, too - so... okay, okay... we were probably exceeding the maximum structural rating of the hot tub, and when combined with the weight of our burbling human broth water we were probably only moments away from collapsing the entire scene down on top of the mountainside crunch-n-muncher anyway… gravity has never been particularly… kind… to me…

BRILLIANT!

These inspired moments are like glittering little amethysts in field after field of the day-to-day brain poo that is my life, but when they strike? EUREKA!

"I love you…" I whispered to her.

I looked her in the eye.

She returned my gaze with abject horror. "What are…"

I lifted us both up out of the water.

Adrenaline coursed through my veins.

"Not today, Fuzz Bucket!"

105

I slipped on the bottom of the hot tub.

Gravity reminded me of my proper place in the food chain.

Have you ever seen a large ship launched from drydock? And the tidal wave that sometimes swamps the poor onlookers standing on the pier?

Yeah.

Only this time the thundering tidal wave was man-made.

And our pitch-black furry intruder was standing exactly where the deluge slammed into the mountainside.

I'm not sure my coughing and sputtering and flailing about had anything to do with his hasty retreat. I'd like to think it was more the shock of near-boiling hot human juice raining down on him like death from above.

But somehow… by some miracle… by trying to be the manly-man hero and carry my girlfriend into the safety of our cabin, and instead unleashing a tsunami of reckoning the bear had surely never before or has since endured…

He crashed off into the wilderness with wild thrashing and roaring and all kinds of woody chaos. Birds cackling on the wing. A riotous run.

And we lived.

And he lived.

And I've never been back to Pigeon Forge or in a hot tub since.

KING SIZE IDIOT

Last year I made the decision to accept a friend's invitation to apply for a job at his company working on his team and working directly for him. I trusted this friend; he looked tired and admitted they needed help. He had read a Facebook post of mine lamenting the strange physical attacks I was having, and marveled at my reluctance to seek medical care because I did not have health insurance. I was, and am, blessed to have him as my boss, but even more so to have him as a friend.

The symptoms of the mysterious attacks I was suffering included itchy hives, throat swelling, difficulty breathing, vomiting, liquid explosions of volcanic force from my nether regions, and my heartbeat thundering in my ears. Some people said food allergy. Others suggested food poisoning. My doctor suggested maybe something in my work environment, whether stress-related or otherwise might be to blame, and she asked me if my current job was worth my life.

I had experienced three such attacks in the space of a couple of months, and after I changed jobs, I went almost a year without having another one. I thought the coast was clear. My new boss and friend had saved my life. Life is good.

At the beginning of February this year, Indiana was thwacked with a nice little snowstorm that dumped almost four feet of snow on my brand-new driveway. Being without a snowblower, this meant it was up to me and my rotund forty-one-year-old diabetic body to clear the glacier from my driveway one laborious snow-shovel scoop at a time.

I had just conquered Covid the week before, I had just been dumped out of my latest and greatest romantic relationship the night before, and as an added bonus, I hadn't had anything to eat or drink in over eight hours.

Let's do this! (#midwestsensibility)

After shoveling for over two hours, I came back inside and immediately felt something was… off. I took my hat and gloves and Carhart winter coat off, and my arms were… red.

"No shit, Sherlock – you just moved the weight of an African elephant in snow by hand out there…" I politely reassured myself.

Then the itching began. And the eardrum-bursting heartbeat. And the labored breathing. Oh no, not again… and I rushed to the bathroom to begin the first of three rounds of throat-roasting stomach heaves to birth nothing but futility and tears. My body was furious. My mind was reeling.

I staggered out of the bathroom and collapsed into my bed. I called my mother for help. She said she would be over in an hour after I reassured her, I would survive. I hung up the phone. I closed my eyes.

I woke up sometime later with the feeling I was about to start round four of the Dry Heave Olympics right there in my bed, so like the undiscovered genius I was, I jumped up and started quickly for the bathroom. Porcelain salvation - heed my call!

But suddenly everything went dark No warning. No clue. Just… blackness.

Time passed.

The sound of my bathroom exhaust fan began as an echo, but soon I could hear it as if I was hugging the damn thing. When did it get so loud and… wait, what the...? I could see nothing. This… wait a minute… this didn't make sense. Why was the light off? I remember hearing it click as I flipped it on… but why couldn't I see anything?! What is going on? I couldn't make sense of it all…

Oh. My eyes are closed. I blinked them open and felt my mouth leaking as if I'd been clocked by Mike Tyson himself. I felt a pain in my legs and back, and… why was I laying down on the floor? How did I get here out of my bed?

I sat up and felt the world start spinning. I lost track of space and time and life again. I woke up in a sitting position, head down and drooling all over myself, sweating like a closet prostitute in an Easter Sunday morning church service.

In my brilliant powers of deduction, I figured out *something* was wrong. I steadied myself in the doorway for a moment, then further deduced something was *terribly* wrong when my legs were Jello-tastic. I had been crumpled up on the bathroom floor for… I still have no idea for how long.

I had fainted. Involuntarily. For the first time in my life. And then I fainted again trying to gather myself up off of the floor from the first faint. And all I could think about was getting back into bed.

I steadied myself up into a crouch, and then into a wobbly stand, still

109

not knowing what the hell was wrong with me. It was as if I could see and sense my body malfunctioning, but I was powerless to reprogram it. As an expert I.T. nerd with twenty some-odd years of experience, I had managed to turn it off and on again… twice. But still the show must go on…

My first couple of steps were… successful? Just a few more to my bed, you can do this Nick, yes… almost there… and I would be safe as…UNGH!

The blackness returned. My last sensation was that of my face bouncing off of my end table and plunging head-long, face-first into my mattress. It was a violent tackle Reggie White would've winced away from and shouted "DAMN!!" if he was alive to see it.

Lifetime faint number three had arrived only moments after I had partially recovered from number two.

My brain rebooted this last time only partially.

I smelled my bedroom carpet.

I sensed my intimate spatial proximity to my metal and glass end table, and my Nick-quaked Queen size bed.

My shoulder and face and scalp were bellowing in agony.

I moaned and crawled up into my bed without opening my eyes.

And the world went silent again.

A noise. Like… windchimes in the distance. Like… birdsong on a windy day. Distortion like an Eddie Van Halen guitar solo. What is this… this calling. What's there? Who's there?

"NICK?! NICHOLAS?!"

My mother was calling my name. She arrived almost an hour after my call for help and somewhat prematurely boasted that I would live. She made her way to my room, and I opened my eyes slowly. I told her what had happened. She said my mattress was hanging six inches off of its base.

I asked her for a Sprite. I took a few tentative sips. I felt some mental clarity return. I took a few more sips. I felt some physical strength return.

Soon I made my way out to the living room couch, and after some Club crackers and more Sprite, I was well on my way to recovery. Mom spent the night on the couch just to make sure.

The next day I called my doctor to report the previous day's circus. She scolded me for overexertion on an empty stomach. Dangerously low blood sugar, emotional trauma from the night before, and the physical stress of still recovering from Covid had left me in no condition for the two hours of hard labor I'd put myself through clearing the hundreds of pounds of blizzard's gifts from my property. I wasn't twenty years old anymore; I need to take better care of myself, and so-on and so-forth…

The cost of my lesson? A scraped scalp, a busted-but-unbroken shoulder, eye socket, and cheekbone, and a hangover-like headache I was lucky hadn't been a full-blown concussion. Oh, and a panicked mother's frayed nerves. I had again refused to go to the hospital for the mystery allergic reaction that began the entire derailment.

Several days later I decided to wash my sweat-soaked winter hat, Carhart coat, and gloves. What should I find in the topcoat pocket? A red permanent marker I'd found over a year before in my last job. The date on the box of those markers? 1979.

111

Significance?

It had been almost a year since I'd worn that coat to work. And over a year since I'd put that toxic treasure in my top coat pocket. And sweated profusely in it. And had those same "mysterious" reactions each time I'd sweated so heavily in that coat…

Moral of the story?

All that glitters is not gold.

FECAL SUNRISE

The sun rises on a bitter January Indiana morning, beckoning through dusty mini blinds to the slumbering and blissfully ignorant victim within. Thin, vein-like strands of orange-white light creep silently across the bedroom carpet, climb up the bed, and assault its occupant with annoying illumination and uninvited additional warmth. The dreamer stirs, raging in drowsy haze to remain in his dream world full of white, sandy beaches and glittering oceans of Pacific Island ecstasy. An island goddess clad in a blue and white flower bikini offers him an icy beverage refresher with a seductive and generous smile. The dreamer's flowery lei and chilled Mai Tai suddenly begin to wither and sweat profusely in a sudden rush of damnable heat, as if the devil himself had exhaled to consume them in his own vengeful hatred. Another twitch and the dreamer wakes to find himself thrust into usual morning reluctant, insufferable consciousness. A groan escapes his lips, heart and soul eager to return to paradise instead of braving the frozen morning that is this Tuesday ritual. He rolls over once, tingling remnants of the dream still dancing in his memory, pleading for him to return to his exotic and overly abundant rest. The sun answers the dreamer with steadfast regularity; brighter light and fireplace level heat continue their invasion of the bedroom. The world is awake, and so must he find himself soon.

The dreamer relents and tosses the comforter aside, visions of his glistening Mai Tai firing neurons in his brain to find the nearest commode and facilitate the day's initial and urgent evacuation. Carpet meets bare feet, and the dreamer is reminded of one of life's simple pleasures. Gravity reminds him of its presence in a quick stumble towards the bathroom followed by a hasty crash through the bathroom door and sleepy-eyed location of the white bowl of blessed relief. He is transported back to the beach in a foreign tactile sensation between his toes - moist beach sand. A smile graces his face as evacuation commences, he flexes his toes in an attempt to bury his digits beneath warm sand over the frigid tile floor. The first mental spikes of logic and situational awareness begin asking questions, "When did we dump sand in the bathroom?" and "How can I be standing on cold tile on a Hawaiian beach?" and "Why is the sand gooey and cold?"

In a lightning strike of revelation, the dreamer realizes he is definitely awake, relieving himself on target, and what he is squishing between his toes is not the sand of his drowsy wishful thinking. In a last-ditch effort to abate the swelling panic in his mind, he reaches for the light switch and looks down on the confirmed horror below. A full litter box the night before has afforded the dreamer and his sleepy toes a submersion into day shattering terror via unattended cat matter next to the ignorant, inanimate, and uncaring porcelain existence. The dreamer shrieks a blood-curdling wail of disgust, turning for the shower and its promise of corrected cleanliness.

A labyrinth of similar fecal treasures blocks his path, and he is forced to negotiate the unforgiving terrain in a tiptoe evasive maneuver. Jumping into the tub with furious haste, he wrenches the shower knob all the way to the hot side, squealing as ice cold water sprays his face and further adds to his morning torment. As he desperately disrobes, trying in vain to keep the mess from contaminating his bedclothes.

He can feel the cold water running down his skin and begin to cleanse the disaster his feet have become. The water soon warms, his heartbeat slows, and the soap is liberally applied. His feet and his nerves rejoice in warm and holy sterilization. The rest of his shower is soothingly normal - that is until the realization he must return to the cat poop minefield upon completion – and this time with bare, wet feet.

STREET STUPIDITY

After twenty-two years of driving without one, I earned my very first speeding ticket.

At a busy intersection during an otherwise fantastic, gorgeous early autumn day, I decided to break the law with my best friend from high school/college riding shotgun. A rotund, older middle-aged man in a full-size Cadillac the color of days-old spoiled French Vanilla liquid/semi-solid coffee creamer was in the left lane next to us. The shine on my freshly polished big red dork-mobile did not impress the Caddy pilot in the slightest. As soon as the light turned green, he unzipped his fly and stomped on the geriatric ghetto cruiser's gas pedal, and his decades-old Northstar V8 sucker-punched my stunned HEMI with a quick jab to the driver's side high beam. Because I was having such a good day and was cruising familiar hometown streets with my best friend on a bright, bright, briiiight... sunshiny day, I decided to answer his backhanded challenge and let the HEMI loose. It was over in mere seconds, or so I thought.

Following closely behind the ear-splitting roar of four hundred horses suddenly whipped into maniacal fury, was my mocking, "Uh... buh-bye now!" waving-out-the-window dismissive gesture of phallic triumph, and the creamy dreamy bathtub on wheels disappeared far into my rearview.

"Can you believe it?! What was that guy THINKING?!" My passenger and I traded verbal chest bumps.

Also following behind, FAR behind as it turns out, and completely hidden from me, was a city police officer in a cloaking-device-equipped, stealthy black Dodge Charger. As I was busy bragging about my overkill dominance of an obviously outmatched opponent to my grinning friend in the passenger seat, a royally pissed-off police officer was doing his best to catch up to and corral this exuberant display of wild abandon and reckless disregard for public safety.

I was telling my buddy how I just got stopped on this very stretch of road last week for speeding... and I wasn't even in Sport mode just now... and... I just put midgrade in the gas tank this... morning and... and... and what the?! Where did that black car come from all the sudden...

The white-hot rage I had satiated mere moments before instantly returned. Instead of a testosterone-fueled road rage fire-breathing dragon, this time crawling up my spine was a spiked-climbing-boots-clad lizard of sickening realization that I was so busted. Again. On the same stretch of four-laned, wide-shouldered, nearly empty road of semi-rural freedom I had traversed countless times before without incident in my nearly four decades on this planet. Until last week. And today. I think I've found my Achilles' Heel Trail once and for all...

It turns out, regardless of my personal feelings on the subject of debatable safe speed and clear, dry, idyllic road conditions in late-summer Midwest America, the law says freedom to travel on that stretch of public road is restricted to no more than forty miles per hour. At any time. For any reason.

117

In my attempts to enjoy myself, and entertain my passenger, and bitch-slap the insulting Caddy slugbutt, and let unfurl the mighty wings of my four-wheeled American freedom political statement... I messed up.

I messed up so hard I was convinced my car would be impounded and I was going to jail. This was the end. Farewell cruel world! Blueberries and cherries flicked on, I pulled over so quickly, he never even had a chance to sound his siren.

I think that made him even angrier.

"Officer...Salad Bar" we'll call him was... less than thrilled with me. In fact, I think he was more than just a little upset with me.

"Do you know why I stopped you?" He began his roadside sermon-slash-interrogation. Huffy breathing. Bulging vein on his forehead. Gritting teeth and squatting down in my passenger window next to my statuesque best friend. Both doing their level best to remain calm.

"A little late to the party to prevent the drag race victory there, Sheriff..." was my mental answer. Instead, the stronger angels of my nature won a merciful victory after a hard swallow and an "Uh...no, officer," sheepishly escaped my hideously lying beak.

"Are you SERIOUS?!" his reply rang out. "You had to be doing AT LEAST eighty miles per hour back there and I'd bet it was a lot more!"

He was right. Obviously. I looked down in shame but kept my sunglasses on to prevent him or my passenger from spotting the panicked tears welling up in my eyes.

"Did you see the posted speed limit sign back there?" He asked.

"No, sir..." I began.

"BECAUSE YOU BLASTED PAST IT GOING SO FAST YOU COULDN'T POSSIBLY SEE IT!!" he hollar-rupted.

Inside I grinned at the mental image of a blurry white sign set ablaze in the wake of my Martian Marauder warp-speed-roasting it into oblivion. Outwardly I froze and took another hard gulp of feigned ignorance-slash-terrified humility.

Officer Salad Bar continued in glaring agitation. "This is a major thoroughfare through town with people crossing it on foot all the time and... and... DO YOU KNOW HOW LONG IT TOOK ME TO EVEN CATCH UP TO YOU?!"

More mental pride and high fives from my high school hormones and defeated 'You'll ALWAYS be a loser' demons flattened and engulfed under my burning rubber asphalt shredder. And what do I care if jaywalkers are breaking the law on this accursed lane - no crosswalks means YOU NO CROSSIE! Until I remembered I was in deep shit and better pay attention to the angry man, lest my brain-to-mouth filter fail at this most inopportune moment. A quick glance back at his dumbfounded but still furious facial expression and I was back to full-on swimming pool phallic shrinkage mode...

I felt my testicles ascend as he ripped his sunglasses off and continued his tirade, shouting admonishment after admonishment, and more repeats of a certain phrase that began with the seemingly innocuous but increasingly juicy words "you HAD to be going..." After a few sputters of this venom it finally clicked, as my emotionally supportive passenger later noted:

He hadn't radared me in time.

In his rush to catch up to this raging red rocket he was only able to

119

radar me at the last second and long after the wildly illegal warp speed death-defying deed was done!

This blissful revelation did little to quiet the panic still raging inside of me, when the glory of this momentary victory was shattered as Officer Salad Bar demanded my license and registration and proof of insurance. More venom for the incorrect address on my license and he stormed back into his own (albeit inferior in this particular case) speedy Dodge automobile.

I started breathing again and took a deep breath to try to quell the raging shitstorm that was burbling up inside of me.

My buddy and I confirmed the radar revelation and jaywalking observation mutual mental oasis we had picked up on during the authoritative concussive bullhorn explosions. I apologized to my partner in crime and innocent passenger for the mess we were in.

"All this to prove some point to a dopey Cadillac!" I further lamented.

My friend then spit out the most powerful ten words I've ever heard in our decades of friendship: "If it was me, I'd have done the same thing." I'm pretty sure our friendship is secure for at least a few more decades. And I know you just counted those words as I am indeed counting my blessings as I write this, so... on with the show!

Officer Salad Bar was not so cool when he returned. This time he was staring down at me through my driver's side window, and I wisely sank a bit deeper into my plushy leather driver's seat so as not to provoke any further rage from him. He thrust the paperwork and driver's license at me. I sheepishly plucked them from the bear's paw and was wildly grateful they weren't handcuffs.

"You're getting a speeding ticket today, sir," he began. "I see on your record you've been stopped THREE TIMES this year for speeding, including this very same spot last week and then again today."

I swiftly recalled the other two incidents and how those officers were always berating me from a much more uncomfortable southernly position next to my back window. But not today. Today I had earned a front-and-center ass chewing.

His heaving chest and piercing stare seemed to intensify to their highest levels with the conclusion of his lecture. "You have a speeding problem, sir. These stops are meant as a corrective action. Obviously, the warnings you've been granted aren't sinking in, so you're getting a speeding ticket today for forty-five miles per hour in a forty-mile-per-hour zone. And that is also a courtesy because we both know you were doing at least twice that and probably well into triple digits, and I'm doing you a favor. Now here is your court date here on the bottom of the ticket if you wish to contest this charge, but I wouldn't recommend it because all of our interactions today have been recorded on audio and video including my pursuit and how long it took me to catch you."

My heart sang out the Braveheart theme song as I silently read the ticket. There it was! In black and white from the boy in blue - forty-five miles per hour in a forty-mile-per-hour zone. How furious he must be! How enraged he must be with lava in his veins knowing he had to settle for a paltry five-mile-per-hour infraction! I heard my late father's words ringing in my ears "IF you get pulled over at ANY time for ANY reason, act as dumb as you look and keep your mouth shut unless they ask you a question. Be polite. Be respectful. But be dumb." Gone fourteen years and he's still saving my ass...

"SLOW... DOWN!" Officer Salad Bar's bullhorn was back on duty and snapped me back into reality with an exaggerated twitch. I nearly dropped everything in my lap.

As he turned back towards his cruiser and half-heartedly offered me "have a nice day" tidings, I briefly forgot myself and my predicament and piped up. "What about my incorrect address on my license?" I swear I can hear my father spinning in his urn...

"Your ADDRESS is CORRECT in the SYSTEM!" the clearly exasperated man shouted back. I smiled and thanked him and (silently) my lucky stars, and over-obvi-cautiously used my turn signal to merge back into the traffic lane from the shoulder and set the cruise control exactly on the speed limit as we pulled away.

Lessons learned:

1.) I am an overgrown child behind the wheel of a vehicle. This is not a new condition, nor do I own exclusivity rights to it, nor is the sharpness of my tool to blame for yesterday's events.

2.) I have a road rage problem. Again, the aforementioned riders apply to this super-obvious revelation as well.

3.) I was wrong, I broke the law, I got caught, and I got punished.

4.) I got lucky. Again.

But still I have to wonder where that dog-derp tan Cadillac went to evade that black police cruiser so expertly...

STREET PANDEMONIUM

"Christina Hendricks" or "Rumbles" — 2014 Dodge Challenger 100th Anniversary Edition R/T Plus

It happened again today.

For those of you who don't know me, I own a muscle car. Rather, the bank is graciously allowing me to borrow the hotness until it's paid off and I can legally call her mine. That being said, I try my best to take care of her. Premium dino juice at the pump when it is less than insanely expensive, and NEVER below midgrade under any financial circumstances whatsoever. Mobil 1 full synthetic motor oil, no compromise on that at any time for any reason. Monthly fee unlimited car washes at the local Crew Carwash. Parking as far away as possible from toddlers, shopping carts, Canada geese, and human beings in public places. I don't rub her with a diaper on my days off, but I make damn sure to engage in some windows down, sunroof open, remote country road therapy whenever I can. She is my pride and joy and my most favorite (almost) possession. Rain or shine, snow or sleet, bone chilling cold and soul scorching heat, I drive her daily.

I've often heard life is more about the journey than the destination. In this car I couldn't agree more. I look down in pity at the seemingly endless throngs of commuter class vehicles clogging our American roads. Volkswagens. Kias. Hyundais. Toyotas. Buicks. All minivans. All SUVs (quit fooling yourselves, folks: they're just mini minivans). Pickup trucks (farm implements). All of those vehicles out there without souls (namely Kia Souls. What the hell are those ugly things? Rolling toasters!). No wonder nine out of ten drivers on American roads these days are distracted — their vehicles are putting them to sleep!

My hotness has about four hundred horsepower under the hood. What does that mean? Apparently if you lined up four hundred Budweiser Clydesdales and harnessed them all to a semi-moveable object and whipped them with a raucous "HIYAH!!" - that amount of force is an approximation of the power level I have at my right foot's disposal at any given time when the engine is operating. That is my fire-breathing dragon doing everything in its massive willpower to keep from burning rubber around you while you're driving forty-five in a fifty mile per hour speed zone. While you're changing lanes without a signal. While you're merging onto the seventy mile per hour speed limit interstate at fifty, and the unmitigated chaos that results from your inane, grossly inappropriate merging technique. While you're bumbling along blissfully unaware of anything going on around you because K-LOVE is having yet another fundraiser and that lady's life was forever changed because she donated last year, and her husband was miraculously cured of stage seventy eyelid cancer and you need a miracle in your life right about...

RRRRAAAAWWWWWRRRRRRR!!!!!!!!!! For the love of all things holy, there is only so much my barely-beneath-the-surface volcanic road rage can tolerate!

She is beautiful, she is vulgar, and she is a caged beast with the door unlocked one roar away from blastoff every single time I sit and hit that start button. Any message I wish to portray to my fellow road-goers is instantly and loudly accomplished with a blip of the gas pedal. Sure, she's been put in her place a couple of times. A Ford Raptor pickup truck (still just a farm implement). A 2017 Camaro SS. Porsches. Corvettes. But ninety-nine times out of a hundred we find a way to get the upper hand over everyone else in the idiotic warfare that is traveling on American roads.

But she was threatened one morning. It wasn't my life I was concerned about. Instead, I was worried about our adversary and what might happen to him should his arrogance dare crinkle my Precious.

Nonchalant commute at first, only minutes into the morning adventure. Why not duck into the car wash since I'm dropping forty dollars a month for the unlimited privilege, and we're not supposed to get any rain until next week and this Journey song is really feelin' good right about now and turn signal on and... HOLY HELL A FLASHY BLACK METEOR NEARLY DINOSAURED US TO

KINGDOM COME!! WHAT WAS THAT SONIC BOOM?!

It was an oil-slick black fourth generation sharkface Camaro. Lowered. Cragar rims. Tinted windows. Aftermarket exhaust. AutoZone LED fog lights. I spotted him approaching the turn from the opposite direction I was headed. Male driver. Frowning. Slight upper lip curled in semi-snarl. Single hand fearlessly protesting the ten-and-two two hand rule at a swagger-licious high noon position, ready to rock hard that first generation airbag steering wheel in vicious turning motion at the first sign of straight-line trouble.

Every time these guys try to act hard around my muscle car, I pity them. These cars are a dime a dozen here in the Midwest, and from what I've seen in the past twenty-some-odd years, it's the exact same demographic piloting them. It's like every single driver out there in these rolling chumbuckets has something to prove, and how DARE you mock them! Rolling short man syndrome on parade. *"THIS* is a CHEVROLET *CAMARO!"*

Whatever his problem was, he didn't feel it was necessary to legally yield to me during his left-hand turn nearly into my driver's side door. I had signaled, I had the right of way, I had to thunderstomp my cold brakes, so he didn't end us both. Death at forty miles per hour. What an embarrassment. To seal the deal, he squealed his tires and shat road buckshot all over my front end as he continued his phallic display of disregard for traffic laws, common decency, and sleepy seven a.m. Wednesday morning commute civility.

My hair trigger, white-hot molten road rage instantly Incredible Hulked, and the normal feather foot that is my right bottom groundling appendage when riding this dragon turned into a USAF depleted uranium A-20 Warthog Vulcan cannon shot of unbridled fury.

The aftermarket exhaust on my own rolling testicle wailed out its righteous rage at ear-piercing, peaceful morning shattering decibels and all four hundred Clydesdales were thumped into vengeance mode in less than a second. I made such a spectacle of the ordeal there should've been SWAT called out and maybe even the National Guard. This is as close to homicidal rage as it gets without actually murdering someone, folks… and that's exactly what I wanted to do to this weeping assbag of a showoff circumcision accident gone horribly wrong. Can you imagine that pipsqueak weakling two-hundred-horsepower on-his-best-day wagging his man cannon at me as if my dragon was completely toothless and only looked like it should be avoided? Have you ever seen what happens to a starving dog when you wag a package of rancid bacon in its face?

It was mere moments before my crimson lightning bolt had tail-slapped the shark-face into total submission, thundering… roaring… BLASTING past him like there was no tomorrow. And there almost wasn't. It's easy to lose your temper and shake your fist or other vulgar gestures in a supremely offensive protest at your fellow taxpayers, road warriors, and breathing colon polyps; it's harder to do so while maintaining control of an enraged bucking broncho of a muscle car with too much NA-NA.. nah NAH! for its driver's own good. You see, blind rage in human beings has the nasty little side effect of causing tunnel vision sometimes, and while I was focused on whipping the impudent little Chevy gelding, I wasn't focused on the huge curve in the road we were approaching at breakneck (read: maniacal) speed. The moment my eyes went from ocular murder mode and back into vehicle steering responsibility, the white-hot rage turned into white-hot panic, and I glanced down at the Sport mode button on my console that is supposed to be engaged for revenge operations like the one I was currently waging war in. It wasn't.

The two-lane curve is tricky at the posted thirty-five-mile-per-hour speed limit. On dry pavement. With noonday sun. Staying in your

127

own lane. Unopposed. Under control.

From the left lane I took a millisecond to glance down at the speedo, you know… so I could brag about my win to the demons and devils in whatever Hell I was destined for. Speedo report: well over twice the limit - my eyes beholden damp, dawn pavement. And the stupid black Camaro trying for a comeback in the right lane.

Now, as far as physics go, I never took a class in high school or college, but experience has taught me when you throw an automobile into a violent maneuver such as attempting a thirty-five-mile-per-hour curve at almost three times that speed, no matter how muscled your muscle car is, you aren't going to make that turn. Furthermore, you will turn the steering wheel to the left, your front tires will indeed turn, but the car itself will continue on its fantastic voyage in a nearly straight line through the curve, most definitely out of your lane, and straight nuts into whatever vehicle, object, or animal is in the right lane on your way off the road and into oblivion. The laws of physics are simple: they state you are an idiot and deserve to be punished and/or killed for your vehicular lunacy. Higher brain functions completely blasted away by rage and panic, I tightened my grip on the steering wheel, stood on the brake pedal, prayed to a God I recently denounced as nonexistent or at least completely disinterested in little ole' me, and braced for the inevitable tragedy.

My hotness came specially equipped with several options. Something called a "Super Track Pack" (totally not making that term up, blame Dodge) which included larger brakes, lowered and beefier suspension, wider wheels, performance tires, and an engine management computer that is apparently just lying in wait for asinine attempted death maneuvers just like this one. I'd like to think Dodge engineers realized that overgrown children such as myself would be ill-prepared to properly control such a rambunctious rocket that is my car and their poster child celebration of one hundred years of Dodge automotive glory. After all, these are the same people/sorcerers that brought us the Dodge Hellcat, a seven-hundred-seven horsepower factory moonshine gulp on wheels, and the even more insane Dodge Demon with 840 horsepower that was banned from NHRA drag strips for being, and I quote, "too fast." If they can figure out a spell that makes these things rip pavement up in boulder-sized chunks in a straight line, surely they can find a way to protect me from myself when I try to turn my paltry little four-hundred horsepower logic guillotine, right?

And that's exactly what happened. The brake stomp, double-fisted steering wheel assault, and praying, coupled with some anti-momentum field generated effect from some as-yet-undiscovered time, energy, or matter distortion generator located SOMEWHERE in my car caused it to squat down like a bobcat stalking its prey, lunge forward into the curve with reckless abandon, tires squealing like they were being William Wallaced on the rack, chicane-like swish-flip waa-laa potato cannon spud launch out the other side of the curve like it was just another day at Laguna Seca or the Nürburgring. Maintained my side of the road, if not my individual lane. I haven't located my testicles in the aftermath of this stupid stunt either, but I'm pretty sure they're hiding somewhere inside some deep, dark recesses of undiscovered warmth and safety just like that undiscovered miracle engine somewhere in my car. After I regained consciousness and checked all of my mirrors, I saw the Camaro so far behind me it looked like a stray puppy tripping and falling all over itself to catch up to its new owner. I started breathing again and also double checked my window slits for any law enforcement presence that may have been a little less appreciative of my reckless fighter jock bravado, and (thankfully) no such luck.

What's the lesson in all of this? I was hoping it would make a difference to that little black Camaro that got schooled, but as I was pulling into the car wash it roared past in continued defiance and a hollow overtake victory.

What just took you probably several minutes to read took less than ten seconds to happen in real time. That's how fast stupidity rears its ugly head. No matter how big my engine is, no matter how high my fuel octane or horsepower or throttle expertise, I'll never outrun my own capacity for vehicular stupidity. And what's worse: I know of my potential for it, my ability to negate all higher consciousness and turn into an adrenaline fueled war child with a loaded weapon in a world full of innocent bystanders and people who feel no rage when they're cut off by lesser mortals in sub-par vehicles.

I got lucky this morning. Someday that luck will run out. And I hope it's just me that gets ended. The worst part is I'm only one drop in an ever-growing sea of road rage idiots out there. I'm making efforts to relax and enjoy the ride.

But then I get in my car and drive around on public roads and the donkeys are outbreeding us conscientious drivers and I just want to travel eight miles in less than forty-five minutes and this jackass in a Scion is straddling both lanes and…and…

DODGE THIS

Looming, lumbering, and large in my rearview it swerved.

Chunky butt Dodge minivan clad in white, all windows tinted darker than night.

We both changed lanes to avoid a garbage truck stopped in the right lane at a stoplight.

Why lean to the Left when you can drive it instead?

Except this morning it's road war instead of vote war...

Chunk style proceeded to ride my back bumper like Kurt Russell at full gallop in Tombstone.

This was okay for the first few seconds - of all people I, myself, understand conveyance impatience.

But soon enough the novelty of not seeing headlights and only hood and windshield wipers in my rearview wore off.

As did the rest of my patience.

By the next major intersection, I had reached my limit and immediately following the traffic light exchange of stop-go negotiation, my brake lights illuminated the otherwise pitch black interior of the overgrown tuna can.

This was met with instant hard braking by Dodge cream corn transport and the swinging rearview noose trinkets waving violently as the walrus wallowed told me: message received.

As did the driver's repeated middle finger salutes.

I'm not going to lie - since this human's favored communication medium was just repeatedly and passionately reinforced, I lowered myself to his level and returned the greeting.

Not once, not twice. But even as his gnashed teeth were bared and his frothing, foam-covered lips were peeled back in caveman fury, I managed to communicate a third time by rolling my window down and extending my greeting far above my roofline in freezing skin fashion.

As we rounded the next corner and his rage was still insatiate incarnate, I spotted my true salvation - one of the city's finest parked alongside the highway, standing out of his SUV cruiser, radar gun in hand, pointed directly at us.

My feathery salute instantly turned into pointy, pointed vindication as I highlighted a much heftier consequence of Chunk style's impatience, followed by a thumbs up to the officer who probably saved me (or bulge butt) from gristly road rage expiration.

The van followed me almost the rest of the way to work, turning at the last moment. As our paths separated, I felt relieved and realized for all of the throttle jockeying and brake pedal stomping and lane wand weaving I had done to separate myself from the NASCAR wannabe he still managed to stay right behind me until the very end.

Life... as a journey.

STAFF APPRECIATION DAY

The yearly staff appreciation day rolled around again. A feigned, heartfelt gesture from the completely-disconnected, albeit good-intentioned staff morale committee and lower middle management representation for a major U.S. university school of veterinary science. The weekday before the start of fall semester, it's meant to lift spirits before an onslaught of "the future" returns to campus and brings unholy ignorance and unrealistic expectations (read: "hopes & dreams") with it. A chance to smile at one another, play "getting to know my coworkers" games, and froyo, jelly beans, punch, and treats for "the family." A reminder that "we're all in this together" and there's no "I" in "team," and a momentary break in the serious business of saving lives — four-legged, beaked, scaled, furried, or otherwise.

It always reminds me of the Aunt Irma visits/Project Icarus episode of The I.T. Crowd if anyone remembers that gem of a BritCom.

Anywho…

MY I.T. Crowd made its way up from the dungeon and down from the attic to partake in the revelry. Crawling outside into the toxic sunshine where our pasty white skin and social anxiety disorders made for awkward interactions and even more painful forced conversations, an unfortunate but tragically accurate feeling of "us vs. them" was palpable and made moods nervous and strained. Oh sure, smiles and affability abounded, but no sooner had we arrived did the true onslaught begin: "Hey! Quick question…"

If I had a dollar for every time I heard those two words throughout my day, I could've retired merely a year into my twenty-odd year I.T. hobby and career. I am the frontline and public face for the I.T. group on the hospital side — and if you're thinking "oh how cute! Animal hospital I.T.! That sounds like FUN!" let me help you with some perspective:

Four-hundred-plus desktop computers, laptop computers, tablet computers, workstations, printers, label printers, mobile pharmacy cabinets, diagnostic imaging modalities, and every employee's personal cell phone and laptop and tablet spread out across four hundred thousand square feet of large animal hospital, small animal hospital, and a satellite equine hospital facility ninety miles away. Departments include ER & ICU, Oncology, Radiation Oncology, Diagnostic Imaging (including Nuclear Medicine), Ophthalmology, Surgery, Neurology, Dentistry, Dermatology, Urology, Cardiology, Psychology, Pharmacy, Clinical Pathology, Endoscopy, Community Practice, Equine Community Practice, Shelter Medicine, Central Supply, Reception, Administration… and a partridge in a pear tree. All human healthcare grade equipment. And if you think crawling under desks is disgusting in an office environment just imagine doing so in facilities where puddles and piles of muckderp are a gross reality twenty-four-seven, three-sixty-five.

My Hospital Information Systems I.T. group consists of six members. Manager, Database Architect/Engineer, Network/Server/Backups Admin, Web Programmer, Trainer, and myself as Technical Support Analyst/PACS Administrator/Purchasing/On Call & Remote Support. We do our best to keep the ship afloat despite overwhelming odds and crumbling, cramped, often grossly inadequate facilities, staffing, and major public university "oversight." I myself have been on call twenty-four-seven, three-sixty-five for five years straight. Our end users are wholly dedicated to saving lives, and we are deeply dedicated to enabling their daily miracles.

The academic portion of the college has its own I.T. group, and even some student employees. Administration has decided we will soon be merging with them, despite our protests and pleas for self-control, glaring academic vs. healthcare I.T. environment differences, budgets, etc., but I digress and will circle around back to my original point.

We beg and plead for our admittedly overburdened end users to call, submit tickets, emails, and/or page me for their technical support needs, I.T. questions, comments, and/or concerns. Yet ninety to ninety-five percent of my day is dropping everything to respond to questions, catastrophes, and requests from people who see me walking by and remember the emergency I.T. need they didn't notify us about any other way until "Oh! Glad I caught you!" or "Did anyone call about this?" or "Did you fix that yet?"

I was at the staff appreciation function for ten minutes. In that time, I got six questions and support requests. And zero helpings of froyo. I sounded the retreat and returned to the relative safety of my shared and stupidly cramped office to address the most recent round of impending I.T. doom.

Does anyone else have the same or similar experiences in their careers? This is why I constantly argue I.T. is a career about people more than machines. Computers would be perfect technology if it weren't for the pesky humans using them!

CORONA ISOLATION: 2020

Isolation.

The title of a book I have never read has been floating around in my brain bucket all week, banging against the sides of my skull and with every collision the ring of irony clangs louder and louder:

"Love in the Time of Cholera."

According to the little research I've done, this is supposedly a novel published in the 1980s about unrequited love, missed opportunities, sin, heartache, and ultimately: redemption.

Admittedly, I have nothing but time to find out for myself what the book is all about. However, thanks to authors with names like Bradbury, Orwell, Thoreau, Vonnegut, and Thompson, I find my list of must-reads growing faster than my list of have-reads even in a time of worldwide pandemic that encourages social distancing and exaggerated personal space as a method of outright species preservation.

Translation: I've got a lot of books to read. And plenty of time and opportunity to do it now. But I've got a lot of books to read. This one may never make the list.

My consciousness tiptoes along the book title words in rhythm like Ray Charles' left hand on the Wurlitzer during the intro to "What'd I Say"; "love in the time of, love in the time of, doot-doo da doo-doot…"; but then the last word is a rimshot that brings the thought into an abrupt end: "cholera."

Endless news stories. Endless conversations. Everyone's talking about it. Everyone's behaving differently because of it. Economic devastation. Fear, sickness, anxiety, depression…

"Love in the Time of Corona"

I am not a fan of this 2020 vocabularial spin called "social distancing." Let's call social distancing what it really is: isolation.

Nations and states and cities and health organizations around the world are ordering, instructing, begging, pleading, threatening (see: the Philippines) the human population to protect each other by isolating ourselves from one another, with the only caveat being "travel for essential needs only." The problem I have with this concept is that leaving people to their own mental facilities to judge what is truly "essential" is wicked folly; I've seen some of these people. I've driven on the same streets with some of these people. I've helped some of these people with computer issues. I've seen what some of these people do when a weather report mentions snow or severe weather and how the true storm hits toilet paper, milk, and bread aisles in the grocery stores. One change "the Rona'" has already made in me - I will never again saunter past a shelf of TP at the grocery store without performing a mental equation:

Available grocery $$ (+/-) available storage space ÷ by the probability of impending donkey stampede due to inclement weather and/or global Chicken Little human extinction prediction(s) =

"Yes, stupid - just buy more toilet paper."

Is there an argument to be made for actually trusting people to do the right thing and alter their behavior to preserve the very species they are members of? Can we trust adult human beings to take "suggestions" and "recommendations" instead of ordering or commanding them to save themselves? Skyrocketing death tolls around the world would be my argument against such a bold miscalculation of global social intelligence so far...

I'll spare you any further review of the reality all but the most backwards, cut-off, or grievously afflicted dullard is all too familiar with these days and simply ask:

What does "Love in the Time of Corona" mean to you? How are you dealing with this crisis? Not just emotionally, but physically?

What are you actively doing to maintain any semblance of order and life in a time when pandemonium seems to be reigning supreme and one minute we're supposed to be wearing masks and the next we're not but oops yes we are and oh look another cruise ship full of death and how about a diesel locomotive coming within three football fields of ramming a US Navy hospital ship and striking grocery shopper workforces and respirators and Governors and presidents, OH MY!

I am a native Hoosier who, in any other year, would be eyeing the calendar with excitement instead of dread, watching it inch closer to that normally glorious month of May that is a special time in this state but will be crickets this year coming from a certain paved modern marvel a few miles south but forever close to my heart and the cherished Indy 500...

Cable TV is not helping me. I find the innumerous commercials from car manufacturers and car dealerships and insurance companies and restaurants and furniture companies offering their "support" and hollow platitudes of "we'll get through this together and, oh! by the way, keep buying our stuff - we're altering the deal!" None of it is anything but panic mode shell games even more insulting and pedantic than usual. Anyone who knows me beyond a certain status knows of my acidic loathing for advertising in general, but this is next-level suck using emotional appeals during a true planetary crisis to continue to pawn your junk off on humans trapped in their own homes.

So, how am I solving this stress?

1.) My first suggestion is, as always, cut the cord and say goodbye to commercials forever. If you can possibly live without network and/or cable TV, for the sake of all humanity please do so and get your news online like the rest of us in the 21st Century. Breaking news! and pandemic preaching and endless bombardment of doom and gloom and then [national fast-food chain] is "thinking about you right now" so, by all means, pepper your panic with pounds of emotional eating of truly terrible foods and they'll be super awesome to you and deliver their artery death to you for free and… and… CLICK! Turn it off!

2.) Communication by phone, online, or the rare in-person check-ins with friends and family. This is by far the strongest thread by which my life is hanging.

3.) I get to go to work five days a week. Seeing human beings in person is an incredible blessing at this time and one I will never take for granted again for as long as I live.

4.) Going outdoors whenever possible. One Friday afternoon, I realized I was able to drive home from work with the windows down and the sunroof open and the radio blaring. This was a gift and in its glory I fully basked, but so is walking outside to get the mail. Standing outside on the patio to breathe in some fresh air and listen to the birds chirping and feel the sunshine on my face.

5.) Turning off the TV/computer/ electronic noise and listening to music. See above.

6.) Attempting to moderate my food intake and FORGIVING MYSELF FOR STRESS EATING when I fail. I was fat and single before Rona; I will be fatter and single-r after her. So be it. This is NOT the time for packing on the pounds AND shame AND self-loathing.

7.) Reading. See above.

8.) Writing. (Thanks for reading, friends.)

9.) Cleaning. Myself, my clothes, and the house, too. Sanitizing physically and soothing mentally.

10.) Remembering the souls and loves that got me through other storms in my past. I have to remind myself that this pandemic is a rough road I have never traveled before, but there have been other rocky roads and trails. There have been other struggles and victories. There have been other trials.

11.) Acknowledging my fear and ignorance about the breadth and depth of this crisis and steeling my determination to get through this the best I can and help as many as I can along the way.

12.) Reaching out and encouraging someone else, and telling them to remember, beyond the craptasic hollow platitudes saturating mass media, that some of us still care and still need and still love them.

COVID COPING MECHANISMS

Coping mechanisms.

I consider myself many things, an incurable cynic among the strongest of my character traits. While this has led me to immediately observe and plan for the darkest of predictions for the most inane of human behaviors, or whatever life usually throws at me, the global pandemic that is the Red Plague of 2020 is an entirely different animal.

To temper this natural grumpiness, I pepper my life with sarcasm, humor, and a razor-sharp wit that can cut through almost any circumstance to find a humorous light at the end of every tunnel.

This is not so with Coronavirus.

Looking at infection models, watching the news, talking with friends and family at some distance and even locally - the fear and danger about this plague is very real and very... here. Anywhere you go from a mile away to a thousand miles away, everyone is talking about it, prepping for it, hoarding, acting like "The Walking Dead" on AMC was a documentary and we're only weeks away from needing Woody Harrelson and Emma Stone to drive around America in abandoned cars re-murdering the infected masses.

My natural cynicism does not save me from my need for social interactions with my fellow potential plague carriers. I once took a work-from-home position, and it was the worst professional decision of my life. It should be no big secret to anyone who's spent more than 10 minutes with me that I'm a people person. It is as much a part of me as my love of Pizza King, fast cars, music, Igloo Frozen Custard, Geeks Who Drink Trivia/Wings at Walt's Pub every Wednesday night, and science fiction or fantasy movies.

How am I coping with all of this social distancing? Admittedly not well.

There are gleaming bright spots, however.

One of my friends started a trivia game online that unites some of my Geeks Who Drinks friends, and it is proving insanely fun and incredibly healing to hear their laughing voices in the midst of all the chaos.

I took an hour's walk outside with another friend last night and her pupper doggo, soaking up the sunshine and gorgeous weather with beautiful company in beautiful surroundings. It was therapy of the highest order. Even a friendly neighbor came out to chat with us at the end of his driveway because we waved. Humanity found in another random human? INCONCEIVABLE!

Another cherished friend dropped off delicious chicken and sausage gumbo for dinner one night this week, leaving the Tupperware container on the front porch and in doing so a reminder of why some people will remain in my heart forever.

I check in with friends and family in-person when possible, but extremely rarely and always maintaining the six-foot neutral zone.

Phone calls over texts, texts over silence. I don't think so many

143

people from so many different lands and cultures will take communication and its sacred place in the human experience for granted ever again. I know I will never again doubt the value of a phone call, text, random greeting card, or an invite for wings and beer or a night out.

My heart goes out to friends who've been afflicted. To those who will be. To those who've lost their jobs and are wondering what's next. And most of all to those and the families of those who will succumb to this modern scourge of viral pandemic.

Because everyone needs another piece of advice from another blowhard with zero medical education from anywhere but the School of Hard Knocks:

Stay home. Did you catch that part? Louder for those in the back?

STAY HOME!

Hug your kids and pups and kits and significant others.

Hug everyone else electronically, or by phone call, or even by snail mail.

Find something to take you away from the madness and give yourself a mental break from the panic and fear and social stupidity that has never been more glaring in at least my lifetime: A book. Netflix. Video games. Discover meme after meme and plaster social media with your internet scavenger hunt cleverness. Learn a foreign language. Submerge yourself in the gloriousness that is Bob Ross and the Joy of Painting. Turn the noise-boxes off. Take a walk. Try to emulate Bob Ross and paint that pesky fence. Take a bike ride. Rediscover the Moody Blues on vinyl. Spring is coming - get a jump start on the attic/garage/refrigerator top that is gathering all the things. Put up the flagpole you've always wanted. Go for a drive -

gas hasn't been this cheap in years!

Find out what really makes you tick on www.16personalities.com

Maybe write some thoughts about life, liberty, and the pursuit during these trying times? The next Great American Novel isn't going to write itself...

Thank an I.T. nerd for being...a nerd?

STOP BUYING ALL THE THINGS. If you must buy, buy local, and buy enough for a week at most and leave some stuff for the rest of us poor fools suffering right along with you.

Thanks for being with me (in spirit) during this global crisis, friends. Take care of yourselves and each other as best you can as remotely as you can. We'll get through this. And we'll all be stronger and closer because of it.

Nick O'Neill was raised among the rolling fields of rural, smalltown Indiana that offered a lifetime steeped in rich, Midwestern goodness. He attended Purdue University for Information Technology and works in the field today. He resides in Lafayette, Indiana, and if he isn't catching a Cubs game, he's sharing drinks and laughs with friends where he adds to the collection of stories in his brainbucket. What free time he has is largely spent serving his feline overlord and roommate, Gandalf.

www.ingramcontent.com/pod-product-compliance
Lightning Source LLC
Chambersburg PA
CBHW061525020726
47502CB00006B/2230